I0780819

Anywhere But Here, Anyone But You

A Novel in Verse

B. Randall

Copyright © 2024 by B. Randall

All rights reserved.

ISBN: 978-1-965794-01-2

No part of this book may be reproduced in any form or by any electronic or mechanical means, including information storage and retrieval systems, without written permission from the author, except for the use of brief quotations in a book review.

Cover by Vanilla Lily Designs

brandallromance.com

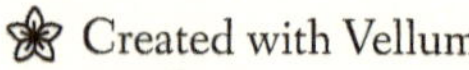 Created with Vellum

For Meghan

Because she's just as much

of a hopeless romantic as I am

And for all the shit

we've survived together.

Here's to the slut and the cowboy,

bestie.

Author's Note

Dear reader,

Thank you so much for picking up this book! It is a novel in verse, which means it's written in poems.

My relationship with this book is complicated. To explain all the reasons why would take days, so I'll just say this: I wrote this book when I was very mentally unwell. My mental health took a horrific turn in 2016 and was almost the end of my life many times before I was able to get help in 2019. I'm honestly really proud of who I am today and how far I've come, even if my mental health is still a daily battle.

During those bad years, poetry was one of the many things that kept me alive. Poetry felt like the only way I could make my voice work. So, I wrote this book. I've written dozens of books, but this will always be the one I'm the most proud of. It represents so much of my life and my pain and my ability to overcome.

Right after I wrote it, I shared it with my agent and my editor. Both of them essentially told me, "I don't get it." There were a million reasons why they didn't want to publish it, so it sat in a drawer for years. And then I started indie publishing, and I told myself that even if no one ever reads it, I had to publish Bethany and Jason's story because it was time to share this part of my heart with whoever wanted to hear it.

Thank you for picking it up.

B.

Content Warning

Anywhere But Here, Anyone But You is a story about domestic violence. There are several scenes depicting physical and emotional abuse. It also discusses cancer, death, and the aftermath of both. It looks closely at alcoholism and other drug use.

If these topics are something you struggle with, I would be cautious about reading further. Take care of yourself.

Anywhere But Here, Anyone But You

Part One
Watters, Ok

This Story Starts With Watters

When I say I have never been anywhere else,

admit that fact with pink cheeks and eyes

that fall easily to the floor, I'm not forming the

same words as my mother who has never been

outside of the south or the middle-aged man

who has never seen the Grand Canyon except

in slippery photographs, slipping right through

his fingers, the person listening with hungry ears

of foreign countries that someone else has visited.

If only. No. That's not what I mean.

I have never crossed outside the state line of Oklahoma,

the box-shaped circumference of my sleepy farm town,

twenty miles or so, the mappable, skeletal outline

of Bay County, its name a simple way to proclaim

its own status as backwoods laughingstock because

there isn't so much as a pond in Watters, OK

and yet the real joke is on me because living

in this town feels just like drowning.

But Really, It Starts With Rachel

Rachel,

my best friend,

whispers her revelation

about the Y chromosome over an

open package of cookie dough

on her bedroom floor.

Her realization

that we should spend

our last summer in Watters

canoodling with the opposite sex,

a tragic I've got a plan

if I ever heard one,

especially when she says

she found me the perfect

over-testosteroned subject.

"His cute friend ordered

a Peanut Butter Xtreme Blizzard

at Dairy Queen."

Rachel knows the importance

of a guy who knows

the importance of chocolate.

Her voice holds the melodic tilt

of a foregone conclusion

as she maps out her proposal,

like that collection of words

should be enough

to convince me

to go on a blind date

with a faceless male figure,

a human ice cream-loving blob.

She swears I don't know him

but if he lives in Watters

that's almost certainly impossible.

A blind date

is not my idea

of a good time.

Nevertheless, I say

"Peanut Butter Xtreme is

pretty boss"

because I am skin

and bone

and no spine.

My Type

Guys

who

listen to Springsteen

wear band tees

and black denim

who

don't smoke

for the sake of their lungs

and the atmosphere

and children with asthma

who

have black and white

photos of obscure objects

scrolling across their laptops

and Polaroids on their walls

from the concerts they went to

this year, last year, two years ago

who

read the New Yorker and Tolstoy

and dream about living in places like

Sydney, Tokyo, anywhere but Here.

Can You Even Blind Date
at a Party?

I don't ask it out loud with my mouth

but it still feels like the words vibrate out

of my brain with each thump of the music

that makes the windows tremble.

My sneaker skids on a mystery substance

and I send up a prayer that it's just spilled beer,

sloshed over the rim of a cup in the hand

of one of the people whose faces I've recognized,

known, since freshman year, middle school,

kindergarten, pressed into the room

like slick salmon in a goldfish tank.

Rachel and I, we met at daycare and so

I know there are no strange faces here.

"Where is he?

How do you even know this guy?"

Rachel's deceptively gentle hand is curved

around a red Solo cup so precisely that I wonder

if the placement of each finger is deliberate.

"A friend

of a friend

of a friend."

"Over by the Sink!"

Rachel's casual demeanor is

enough to convince me that

she is, in fact, an evil mastermind,

the villain of this story,

the man behind the shower curtain,

butcher knife in hand because

she can't be serious.

This must be a trick,

some grand plan blueprinted around

her own desires because

why else would she be nodding

at the only person over by the sink

who happens to be Jason Wells?

Jason Wells

The town of Watters, both famous and forgotten, was constructed at the turn of the century in a square pattern not unlike the state borders it resides within, sans panhandle, cement drying hot in a box around Wells Ranch, sitting right in the middle, the hub of the wheel, the epicenter, ground zero.

Back in the 70s, they filmed some show about cowboys there that still plays on old school syndicated television late at night and ever since, it's been the tourist attraction that's kept the Watters economy alive and booming, earning us a dot on the map,

and most days a person like me, born and bred within Watters' quadrilateral limits, can almost forget about its oddly forgotten fame, until I'm driving by Wells Ranch on my way to work or school or literally anywhere—because you cannot drive in Watters and not drive by Wells Ranch—only to find the road blocked by tourists standing on the blacktop, car doors swung open in the passing lane, cameras pointed up at the metal logo on the gate at the ranch's main entrance—a horse and a cowboy embossed in steel—blocking traffic.

But I digress.

Jason Wells' father owns Watters in that weird macho way that men have ownership over something just by being taller and more muscular than their peers and by having said belief reinforced every time someone stutters in their presence, intimidated by expensive clothes and the scent of large estates full of thousand-dollar furniture.

And so, the Wells boys own this town and everyone in it and well, I'm just not looking to get mixed up in all of that ego.

Whatever Rachel Wants

Rachel gets and so I am dragged

by her scrawny upper arms

—those deliberate fingertips now

leaving deliberate bruises in my skin—

into the kitchen where she positions me

like an actor in a play, X marks the spot,

on a square of tile in front of Jason Wells

who looks like what Michelangelo

was imagining as he chipped away at David,

all hard edges and smooth skin

towering over both of us, more than six feet

of flesh and bone silhouetted in the gold light

of the bulb over the kitchen sink

with eyes the color of what I imagine

Lake Michigan looks like when it freezes

in the winter and stubble on the flat plane of his jaw

with those kinds of hands, you know the ones,

they look rough, holding a beer in a glass bottle

and not a plastic cup like us mere mortals,

so obviously easy in his own skin, tinged red

from the sun and his own blood under the surface

and all of that is just fine and dandy

but he's also wearing a cowboy hat at a party

and cowboy boots and a belt buckle

with a rattle snake on it like he just

stepped out of a sepia photo from a 1920s rodeo

and I can only force three words into my stalled brain,

rattling around like the last pennies tapping the sides

of a piggy bank: oh my god.

Friend of a Friend of a Friend

He must recognize Rachel from the Dairy Queen,

where apparently she went to visit Lauren Barbour,

and who else should be visiting Lauren Barbour

but Justin Dooley and his good pal, Jason Wells.

Justin Dooley has had a thing for Rachel for

as long as I can remember and Rachel has had a thing

for Justin Dooley since she found out he rescued

a turtle from traffic on Monroe Street September of last year,

adopted the damn thing, and named it Spot.

So Jason Wells must remember Rachel's smile

from the Dairy Queen and potentially the part where

she promised to bring a friend to this party

that he could flirt with and smile at and take home,

if she consented to it, and I am not

going home with Jason fucking Wells.

He Smiles

and goddamn it all

if that smile isn't

so beautiful it should

be framed and hung

in a gallery next to

Picasso's and Van Gough's

finest masterpieces.

Bethany, Not Beth

He breathes out my name

"Bethany"

like he's blowing hot air on his hands
to keep them warm.

I shiver
even though that breath
doesn't come close to touching
the surface of my skin.

"You know who I am?"

He graduated from some

fancy private school.

He did not go to

Watters High.

He is nineteen

maybe twenty

depending on the date

of his fortunate entrance

into this universe

and I am barely eighteen

fresh off the Watters High

graduation scene of one week ago.

I am nobody

and Jason Wells

is more somebody

than anybody else

in this godforsaken town.

"Rachel showed me your picture."

Likeness

I know he probably means

my Instagram profile,

the tiny circle-cropped photo

of me and my dog Scout

long dead of liver disease,

but I imagine instead

some tin-metal likeness,

like he's a solider off at war

approximately two hundred years ago,

maybe even a time when

the heels of his cowboy boots

would make sense against the worn down

dust-covered hardwood floor beneath him

and he wouldn't stand out

in a way that makes me wonder

if it's on purpose.

25

Not a Hint

"I'm sure you're really nice

but I'm not interested."

I expect a falling of features,

a gentle downturn of mouth

and the corners of eyes

and maybe even his shoulders

not because I'm so desirable

that Jason Wells should be sorry to lose

a chance with me but because

Rachel delivered certain expectations

on a silver platter and maybe he thought

he was going to get lucky tonight

and maybe if he was someone else,

he might have.

But he continues to smile at me

with just one corner of his pink mouth

and the shape of his eyes squinting in,

not a single twitch of disappointment.

"Why not?"

Why Not

Because

I've been with the kind of boy

who always wants to be in charge

and it gets old being told what to do.

Because

I will not date a boy

who wears a cowboy hat

to a party or at all.

Because

I cannot imagine dating someone

that Rachel picked out for me

like a tube of rose-pink lip gloss

at a department store.

Because

Jason Wells is Famous

and I'm not interested

in my life becoming fair game

to anyone who can't keep their eyes

on their own paper.

Because

Jason Wells is Watters

and I'm getting out of Watters

and never looking back.

The Escape

Why not? is the kind of question

that only a guy like Jason fucking Wells

—who is used to having a concrete reason,

an explanation in the palm of his hand,

for why a girl might be able to resist

the pleasant bow shape of his mouth—

can get away with asking upon rejection

as if he isn't aware that no is exact change.

"I have to go."

The words are so garbled below the thumping bass

and the lyrical rapping of Kendrick Lamar

they may as well be Ancient Egyptian

for all anyone is going to understand

but it doesn't matter because I won't ever

see Jason Wells again except perhaps in passing,

like that one time I drove down Monroe Street

and he was outside the gate of Wells Ranch

leaning against a post, hip cocked, gloves on his hands,

like he was about to do something with rope.

Jason Wells has always been nothing more than

a looming shadow, a far-off silhouette,

a figure in the distance I've never been this close to.

Driving

When I leave the party, I can't even explain

the chaos of my heartbeat and the adrenaline in my veins.

Finding out that Jason Wells was my blind date

is like salt water sucking its way around my eyeballs

and the spaces between my teeth, like someone

has pushed me over and I'm struggling to gain my feet.

So I drive

because I'm not ready to stand still.

But driving through Watters, I'm a silver metal ball

in a pinball machine tilting side-to-side, dinging

against plastic walls and causing a spark that no one will see,

but my eyes are too tired, too achy for

the warm abandoned concrete of the highway

that will lull me to sleep at seventy-five miles an hour

which means I'm circling Watters instead,

around the curves of Monroe Street that I take slowly

in my sleepy caution, past the closed dark windows

of pizza restaurants and grocery stores until,

the streetlights spread out and disappear, leaving

open space for darkness and quiet and vacancy.

I pull over in the empty parking lot of a dentist's office

that I know from when I was a kid and went with Rachel

and her mother for a teeth cleaning, and even though it wasn't

my teeth getting scraped and picked, I still got a grape sucker.

I press my head to the sticky rubber of my steering wheel

and close my eyes, feeling my exhaustion in the marrow

of my bones, like a disease that I'll never be rid of and because

I'll never be rid of it, I start my car and drive home tired.

Home Is Where the Heart Is

I have perfected the art of being gone.

Every night my father leaves

for the depths of some bar

to drink away the realization

that he will never make it to the age

at which his own father died

and slips back behind the wheel

long after midnight,

when the bars in OKC,

where Dad drinks because Watters is dry,

have tripped right past last call,

and steers his way back home

in whiskey-soaked oblivion,

and every night I make sure I'm gone,

sometimes to Rachel's and sometimes

to the shadowy corners of Watters

if Rachel is out of town or busy

or my feet just feel like wandering.

But tonight my carefully crafted sequence of events

has been upturned and I'm standing on the curb

outside my house, where the glow of the lights

is flooding out onto the driveway,

every single one of them on, fluorescent yellow

and orange and white, like the house is on fire,

a beacon on our pitch-black street corner.

I wish it was on fire.

My father's Ford pickup is parked in the driveway,

the smell of cigarette smoke and alcoholed sweat

wafting from the polyester seats through the open window

as I tip toe by like it might try to take a bite out of me.

From inside the house, the clatter of ceramic

breaks the quiet so loud I hear it on the top step.

I bite my lip and bite back bile that rises in my throat.

I stand on our welcome mat, stained an odd color,

not quite brown and not quite red, the whiskey rainbow

of the mud on Dad's shoes and his three a.m. vomit.

I'm supposed to be gone.

There are rules after all:

be gone before he comes home,

come home only when he's asleep.

The plan for tonight was infallible—

go to the party, dance with a perfect stranger,

spend the night in Rachel's room

but Rachel is still at the party and I'm here,

too early, and no matter how many times

Rachel tells me to climb in through her bedroom window

even when she isn't home, on nights like this,

I can never quite force my legs to cross the street

that separates her life from mine.

I imagine Rachel's mother roaming the halls

in the dead of night, stopping in to check on her little girl

and finding some other girl in her bed

like a scene in a horror movie,

a scary story told around a campfire:

Oh daughter, what boring features you have!

Across the street, Rachel's house is dark

like a ship on the ocean

the gentle lights that line the pathway to her door,

making hazy shadows on the grass

and I've been standing here too long in the dark,

not a sound from any direction—no motors or voices.

This is Watters after all.

Silent to the bone,

hushed like a graveyard.

People passing in and out of their own lives like phantoms.

I press my hand to the green paint on our front door

that my mother and I picked out together

from a swatch at the hardware store

one sunny summer afternoon day when the

flowers were in bloom and my father wasn't so angry.

He loved the color, said it reminded him of the forest

behind the house where he grew up in Texas.

Inside, he shouts and she cowers.

It's a practiced dance, performed so many times

I'm tired of paying for a ticket.

And still I have no answer to the question

that burns incessantly in my chest

like hot coals after the fire has gone out:

her or me?

Broken Bones

I put myself in the room

like a crash test dummy,

play through the scenario

that I know step-by-step.

He would lunge for me—always me first.

I suspect it has something to do

with the fact that I'm in perfect health,

young, going somewhere.

But if I'm gone—as I almost always am

when I know he's been visiting the bars,

not taking his meds, a dying man standing

in the center of the living room

where we used to watch

Saturday morning cartoons

and eat bowls of Cap'n Crunch

on our peach-striped couch—

when I'm gone

he goes for her

the only other target

within our four walls

like he is now,

shattering Mom's

favorite Thanksgiving plates

on the kitchen tile.

If I go in, it'll make it worse,

a chance I took only once

and never again.

A lesson learned.

If I go in, Mom will stand between us,

my father's fists and I, and he will

hit her harder than he would have

if I had never been there at all.

Instead of purpling bruises along her arms,

those arms will be broken,

shattered in three or more places.

I'm tired of looking away from X-rays.

Like the phantoms of Watters,

I'm already dead,

floating through this

embarrassment of a life

with guilt gnawing at my

solid, intact, unbroken bones.

But if I go in,

he really will kill her

or me.

Night Life

In the premature hours of the morning,

when the streets are saturated

with moonlight, streetlight, traffic light,

there are still places in Watters that have life.

Gas stations with flickering lights

outside their sliding front doors

and twenty-four-hour burger joints

where only the night-shifters show up

for greasy fries while the moon is high.

Then there are the shadowed places,

where nobody will come looking for you

as long as you're not making noise

or disturbing the darkness,

where you must become penumbra.

The bench outside Watters Public Library

and the fountain in the center of Fraser Park.

The playground behind Watters Elementary

or the bushes outside my bedroom window.

Pretzel Mania

There is a science to twisting pretzels,

to knowing how long they should sit in oil

so the bread stays soft and doesn't crunch,

so the oil doesn't leave pieces behind that are

sour to the tongue, and you have to have

gentle hands when kneading, coated in butter,

and know the right ratio of salt to jalapeño slices.

My favorite are the pretzels with the pepperoni,

washed down with an ice-cold Dr. Pepper,

with a cinnamon sugar pretzel chaser.

A delicacy.

Rachel's favorite—the kind with the parmesan

cheese powder stuck to the butter and salt—

waits for her under the yellow heat lamp because

it's Monday and she always comes begging

on Monday for hot oiled bread on her break.

Her voice is already carrying through the window,

a conversation already well in motion when she

lets herself in, outlined in the doorway by the rays

of the July sun, one silhouette that breaks itself

into two, standing in the echo of the chiming bell:

Rachel and the unmistakable form of Jason Wells,

a Dallas Cowboys baseball cap replacing his

cowboy hat—but really, what's the difference?

And their conversation falls short, like they've

only just realized that other people can hear them

just like I can hear the clopping of Jason Wells' cowboy

boots unironically like horse's hooves until he's

bent forward, distorted face peering in at the pretzels

depreciating as the seconds tick by on the clock.

Sometimes I wish Rachel and I had been the kind

of kids to make up a fake language for moments like this.

I want to tell her in Martian that I don't believe

in summer flings and even if I did, I wouldn't date

someone like Jason Wells and that she should be ashamed

of her appalling best friend behavior, but instead

she smugly takes the pretzel I offer her, with a swish

and crackle of the pretzel bag, a cartoon mascot

smiling up from the logo, and what I really want to do

is smash it into the oil-coated tile floor beneath my feet.

"What do you recommend?"

He speaks so slowly, and I can't help but wonder

what it must be like to have a life that always moves at

your pace, to never have to worry that someone will

speak over you if you don't spit it out.

"The garlic butter pretzel, if you want something savory.

The chocolate chip, if you want sweet."

He orders one of each because he can, I guess

and slips a ten into the tip jar as if it's perfectly natural.

"Have a nice day."

It's my line, but he says it.

47

His phone number is written in big block digits

dark enough to dent the receipt paper

right below his signature.

Rachel

is the beach in summer.

Pacific Ocean eyes,

hot sunshine skin,

wet sand hair,

cherry popsicle-stained lips.

Everybody loves the beach.

Dream Vacation

Rachel is going to the golden land of California

for two weeks/fourteen days/336 hours.

When she told me back in December,

all I dreamed about for a month

was white sand beaches and Disneyland.

Her parents asked me to go with them,

told me they would pay for everything,

right down to the light up Mickey Mouse ears,

but my father said no without hesitation.

Six months I've spent slipping into Rachel's room

when at least three of our parents are dead to the world,

on those nights when I can't be home, can't be seen,

have nowhere else to go but the 7-11 for Big Gulps

of caffeine that keep me high as a kite until the sun comes up

but at Rachel's house, there's

a Minnie Mouse sleeping bag rolled out on the floor,

bags of chips stashed in a box under her bed,

a place I can get some real sleep.

She says she'll leave a key, but I know I won't sleep there

while she's sleeping so close to the Golden Gate Bridge

she can smell its rust.

The refrigerator makes a strange knocking noise,

the deadbolt doesn't always work and the house is so quiet,

it presses against my ears, a black kind of static.

With Rachel there, I feel safe.

Alone? The monsters will creep in.

Pack 'Em Up, Head 'Em Out

Rachel's hugs are like a squid,

wet and full of arms.

Rachel's hugs are always wet

because she won't hug someone

unless she's already crying.

"I'll be okay."

A skeptical eyebrow,

downturned mouth,

tear sliding down the swell

of her sunshine cheek,

blast of a car horn.

"I left the key beside the big root

of the rosebush."

They're gone in a haze

of sticky rubber

and heat lines

floating up off the concrete.

I'm left

standing in the empty driveway,

staring at my own

across the street.

I am okay for now.

Daylight is safe.

Dad works day shifts at the J-Mart

and night shifts at Sandy's Saloon

with his nose buried in a glass of Old Crow.

I can stand here

until I sweat out every drop of water in my body

until I melt into runny egg yolk on the pavement

until my skin turns to crimson leather under the sun.

Night Changes

Rachel didn't know

about the sneaking out,

the wandering of Watters

that my feet did

in those awkward hours

of departed existence,

until she found me

last year

at exactly 3:21 a.m.

in the pharmacy aisle

of the J-Mart,

where she was buying

cherry Nyquil

for her little brother

who has seasonal allergies.

I tried to lie.

"Couldn't sleep.

Needed a few things.

Here for cough syrup too."

cough

cough

But like she always has

since that day on the playground

when we made a spit pact

to be best friends forever,

Rachel smelled my lie

from a mile away,

took me home

like a stray dog,

listened to my sob story,

and refused to let my feet wander

but not even she can stop

the wind from blowing her

all the way to California.

At Night

the air in Watters

smells like the palpable moisture

of a million and one timed sprinklers coming on

as soon as the clock strikes midnight.

The particular quiet of Watters

is just as heavy in the air without being oppressive,

that dead silence broken occasionally

by a semi-truck bolting down Highway 35

and the cicadas, always the cicadas,

chirping, humming, buzzing

but when you've lived here long enough

you hardly even notice it anymore.

The cool air that wouldn't be nearly cool enough

if the sun was out is somehow now just enough

to turn the sweat on my body into a steady chill,

giving me goosebumps along the flesh of my arms and legs.

The best part?

No one saying loudly that they misplaced their car keys,

calling out for their kid to come inside,

speaking secrets in low, muttered tones that register

even when you're trying not to hear,

ordering a pretzel with no salt

and a side of melted neon cheese.

In the quiet, cool, damp air of Watters,

I sit on the park bench outside the library and

pull my feet up onto the wooden slats and

wrap my arms around them as tight as I can,

tighter, waiting for them to break.

I clench my hands into fists, squeeze my eyes closed

burrow my face into the space between my knees

and pray to be anywhere else.

The Bet

Rachel swears that Jason Wells has an observatory in his house

which can't be true because people don't have observatories

in their houses unless they're Lara Croft or a Disney princess,

a sentiment I've repeated something like twelve times

as Rachel texts me from the guest room

of her uncle's house in Burbank

but according to her, and apparently half

the senior class of Watters High,

a dome-like structure can be seen

on the south side of Wells Ranch

as one is driving down Monroe Street,

and people have straight-up Googled this shit.

Rachel is obsessed with the idea,

probably because years of rom-com viewing

have taught her that if a boy has an observatory,

there will eventually be a kiss in it.

So we make a bet:

I will investigate Wells Ranch because tonight,

I will need somewhere to be at two in the morning, so why not?

No observatory means a strawberry cheesecake Blizzard

with added cookie dough pieces for me, and an observatory

means free caramel drizzle pretzels for a week for her.

It's on.

The Problems

1. The "dome" Rachel swears half of Watters

is whispering about behind their hands

while walking down Monroe Street

is, in fact, barely the curve of a shadow, high up,

on the backside of the house, just substantial enough

to warrant this entire masquerade,

and me standing with both feet

in the tall grass, unsure how to proceed

because

2. There is a fence around Wells Ranch.

It is low and easy to climb but it is there nonetheless,

made of tightly strung metal wire that's red with rust,

and I feel certain this is the night that I will finally

see the inside of a jail cell at the Watters Police Station

because

3. I have somewhere between my house and Wells Ranch

apparently lost what was left of my braincells,

the ones not eaten away by butter fumes and bad TV,

because I just step right over that fence and find myself on

PRIVATE PROPERTY to see if Jason fucking Wells has an

observatory, like I give a shit

and

4. I keep waiting for an alarm to go off or to get caught in a

booby trap, a room of lasers that I'll dodge with nimble feet.

Any minute now, a pit will open beneath my shoes,

presenting me with rows and rows of gleaming alligator teeth,

but I am only met with the acrid scent of horse manure,

and

5. I still can't tell if it's an observatory, even up close,

right beneath its dark half-moon arch.

The pictures online that I Googled—because I had no clue

what an observatory looked like from the outside

and wouldn't I look stupid if I said it was one

and it turned out not to be, like anyone would ever know—

showed an opening in the top,

like the split of an airplane hangar,

and this dome definitely has no splits

that I can tell from the ground.

It's just a dome. It could be anything: a silo, a turret,

some kind of special Watters vintage architecture,

and so

6. I climb the dome.

Don't ask me why.

God only knows.

And

7. I make it a quarter of the way up before I fall

and land on my ankle which twists and rolls and aches,

and I smash hard into the cool grass.

8. I'm trying to stand, trying to move myself

by brick and plaster and the pure force of my will

not to die here, under a mystery dome,

amidst the weeds of Wells Ranch

when I hear footsteps.

Wells Ranch

"How did you know I was here?

What are you even doing up?"

Jason Wells' ranch-themed kitchen

has spurs for cabinet handles

and wood grain painted the color

of a barn in a children's book

where a cow, a sheep, and a pig

all live together in harmony,

bunking together in the hay,

and it could also be the color of blood

as soon as it leaves the body,

before the air turns it a shade of chocolate syrup.

"Security cameras.

Insomnia."

And I am the world's biggest dope

because of course they have security cameras.

I can only imagine the uber fans,

the ignorant selfie-ists, the many Jason Wells admirers

that climb over that fence that's not even barbed wire.

I shift and wince.

I know it's not broken, know the distinct crack of a bone

as it snaps, but God it feels like it—

shooting pains and stretched tendons

and a kind of weakness I could do without.

"Should I take you to the hospital?"

That would be an emphatic NO

as I could only imagine what would happen

if I had to explain to my father,

sloppy on cheap whiskey, how I got this injury

and how it would probably result in much worse ones.

"I'm fine.

Thanks for the coffee.

Sorry for trespassing."

The Only Thing I've
Learned About Jason
Wells

is that he doesn't back off.

When you tell him you don't want to date him,

he buys pretzels from you

and leaves his number on the receipt,

a number you will never ever use

and when you hurt your ankle

and say you don't want to go to the hospital,

he crouches in front of you

takes your ankle in his warm hand

his calloused hand

his cowboy hand

and starts to roll it

in a sharp, circular motion

pressing his fingertips into the tender skin

and the aching muscles

and the bruised bones

and you have to bite back a gasp

because you can't remember the last time

you were really touched by anyone.

Maybe almost a year ago

by Corey Sutters,

who kissed you and slipped his fingers

under the hem of your shirt

under the bleachers at the homecoming game

and now you're pretty sure you're turned on because

it's Jason fucking Wells

and even if you hate his stupid cowboy hat,

which is noticeably not present,

and the fact that he has a real-life ranch

you are not blind

and therefore, are aware that he is painfully gorgeous,

like that kind of gorgeous

that makes people crane their necks on the sidewalk,

and now the kitchen is ten degrees warmer

than it was a second ago

and you might be on the verge of

honest-to-God moaning

when he releases my foot so suddenly

that I'm jarred out of my own shame

and looks up at me from where he's still kneeled

like Prince Charming in the flesh,

for Christ's sake, and says

"Why were you climbing

the side of my house

at three in the morning?"

The Real Lie

I suppose I have the option to lie

but what's the point?

He might as well know the kinds of things

they whisper about him at the high school,

at the pretzel shop, at the pool parties.

"I have a bet with Rachel

that you have an observatory

because apparently everyone in Watters

thinks you have an observatory."

It, of course, sounds downright idiotic

when I give the words air,

let them come out of my mouth

as actual vowels and consonants,

but it's not like I was the one

driving down Monroe Street imagining

Jason Wells stargazing shirtless at midnight

in the first place. Quite the opposite.

"An observatory."

I press my lips shut,

superglued against each other,

because I will not pry anymore.
I will not question Jason Wells

about his life, his existence, his home.

"The dome is just for looks."

Jason Wells, six-foot-two at the very shortest,

in jeans and a Houston Astros shirt

and red socks and messy hair,

is staring at me in that way

that says he's trying to figure me out,

eyes pushing past the top layer of my skin.

But I am no lab rat and so I keep my mouth closed.

Jason is used to stubborn animals, after all.

"I should be going."

His socked feet follow me down the hall

in a disturbing child-on-Christmas-morning kind of way.

There are some things you should never see,

like the richest guy in town in

fire engine red ankle socks,

his long arm reaching out for the door

before I even get there,

precisely the wingspan of a pterodactyl.

"Have a nice night."

His words are liquid cement spilled around my feet,

stopping me solidly halfway in and halfway out

of the Wells Ranch homestead.

He stands in the foyer of his mansion,

hands in his pockets,

eyes heavy and a shit-eating grin firmly in place.

I feel like I've been mowed down by a semi

by that smile and those socks

and that dome.

Going Home

Sometimes,

remnants of broken dishes,

knocked over furniture,

smashed picture frames.

Sometimes,

my mother still crying

behind her closed door

when the sky is still gray,

long after Dad has passed out

on the couch

or in bed

or in the bathtub.

Sometimes,

nothing.

Sometimes,

complete quiet,

everything as I left it,

maybe even cleaner,

like the explosion has shocked

the dust from the shelves,

the dirt from the kitchen floor,

the crumbs of food from the table.

Sometimes,

my father still awake,

still rampaging,

still a bull in a too-small pen.

7-11

My favorite after-hours place is the 7-11

on Monroe and Fifth because Polly and Ryan

run the graveyard shift and they let me eat my weight

in hot dogs that are about to meet the trash can.

At two thirty a.m., when the cicadas are particularly loud,

I'm eating a fully-loaded all-beef hot dog

dripping with nacho cheese

as Polly tells me about the customer

who dropped his Slurpee this afternoon,

the wild cherry smell of it still sticky on the floor

but then Jason Wells' cowboy boots are clomping

across the floor with the tiniest hiss of leftover cherry

Slurpee beneath them.

Polly takes one look at him and stops talking

and I stop laughing because the last time

I saw those snowstorm-in-summer eyes,

Jason was massaging my foot

from the speckled tile of his kitchen.

"Thought I might find you here."

I don't miss the way those words mean he was looking for me

but I hope he misses the way I have a glob of cheese

in the corner of my mouth that I can't lick away

for fear of drawing attention to it.

"Not sure what you mean."

Liar, liar, pants on fire.

"How's the ankle?"

I'm counting change like a senior citizen

in line at J-Mart to pay for the hot dog I ate for free

just to give my hands something to occupy them—

anxious puppies falling over themselves,

positively trembling with nerves and something

I'm hardly qualified to put a name to—

when Jason's plastic credit card

clatters on the counter and I immediately push it back,

satisfied at the way it squeaks as it slides

and my exact change lands beside it in a heap

of quarters and dimes and pennies.

"It's fine.

Thank you."

Jason's elbow as it rests on the counter

is obviously meant to be casual but in this 7-11,

he looks about as casual as a rhinoceros in a henhouse.

"Are you often at 7-11

in the middle of the night?"

Two a.m. is hardly the middle of the night.

Chin high. I am practiced at feigned confidence.

He knows he's got me, that much is obvious

from the slight curve of his mouth,

the lift of one eyebrow, so knowing.

"Let's go for a drive."

An Assessment of Jason Wells' Truck

It

is the size of a small aircraft and

most likely impossible to miss as it

lumbers through town with black rubber

wheels that are taller than me. In fact,

it

is much too big to be anything but an

industrial vehicle, a tax write-off, I'm sure,

used for towing other vehicles or herding cattle, but

it

smells like new car in that completely artificial way,

those cardboard air fresheners, shaped like

pine trees that cost the change you can find wedged

between your seats, and

it

has hay scattered on the floorboard,

a pair of boots in the cab,

dirt streaked down the side of a back seat,

George Jones playing from the speakers.

It

means Jason fucking Wells

is such a fucking cliché.

Cute Things and Blue Things

Jason Wells takes me to a twenty-four-hour cafe near 75

that I've never been to because it's outside of Watters

and the furthest outside of Watters I have ever been

is the Christmas tree lot off the highway—and never alone.

I order blueberry waffles and curly fries.

He orders coffee without cream or sugar.

Watches me like I'm going to change form

any minute, transform into an eagle

or perhaps a demon come to drag him to Hell.

"Did you know that a woodpecker

opens its eyes between every peck?"

I close my eyes and stretch my neck in some odd

imitation of a pecking bird and then open them again,

try not to focus on his blank look while I perform

a demonstration of something I saw in slow motion

in a documentary when I was in middle school.

"And their tongues basically travel through their brains.

I mean, if that doesn't prove the existence of God

then I don't know what does."

Jason's blue eyes also prove the existence of God.

I cram waffles into my mouth as his silence

stretches out in front of us, the beginning miles of a marathon.

"The cutest animal in existence is a slow loris

whose bite is so poisonous that it's illegal to own one.

I think that's telling.

That God would make something so cute so dangerous."

I have never been one to associate colors with people,

like auras or whatever, but Jason is blue

from his eyes to his ankles.

"Most cute things are."

Fear Of Missing Out

What do you think is going to happen?

is a question people would ask me

like no one had ever gone home early

just to hear the stories after

of the things they missed.

Like an infant,

I would fight to stay awake,

blinking heavily during dinner

while my parents spoke low,

resting my head on the table,

trying to be part of the fun

while I slept,

a born multitasker.

Always the last person to leave,

always the last to walk away,

slowly, just in case

someone changed their mind.

I evolved,

became a night owl,

a particular species.

Long after the world fell asleep,

I was awake, exhausted,

refusing to yield.

Music is better at night,

when you can play it softly

and still hear all the words

and the silence between the chords

doesn't seem so bad

in the violet hour

until it's broken by the

specific slam of a screen door.

When Dad started drinking,

I started praying

to miss everything.

Knight on White Horse

I know why Jason brought me here

and Jason knows I know

and I know that Jason knows that I know

but it's not going to happen.

I know guys like Jason Wells.

I know exactly what he wants:

to save me.

This is the part of the movie

where I explain the root of my insomnia

with a quirky monologue about night terrors

or an obsession with infomercials

or a desperate desire to know

the taste of the world at night.

I hand him the seeds to root

deep in the soil so he can watch

while I sprout from my ashes

or some such shit,

but I don't have insomnia

just some shitty father

and I am not alive and breathing

for Jason's amusement

and his hero complex.

"These waffles are to die for."

I imagine him examining my comment,

annotating it with a red pen

like a college English professor

digging into Dickens.

Could those words point to suicide?

Or perhaps bulimia?

Should he hand me off to a clinic?

Or a hospital? Or a therapist?

Wipe his hands on his jeans

and then pat himself on the back

for doing such a good job?

"Don't suppose you'll tell me why you're

always roaming town

in the middle of the night."

Ding ding ding.

And here I thought there would be subterfuge,

dancing around the subject,

beating around the bush,

but no, he just comes out and says it.

"Don't suppose I will."

Hereditary

Jason's father,

Malcom Wells,

once came to a Watters High

homecoming game,

the crowd foaming at the mouth

over the game,

which we won,

and Wells Sr.'s presence,

which made us feel like we won,

and when the game was over,

my car wouldn't start,

a dead battery,

and like the dictionary definition

of chivalry,

Malcom Wells jumped my car

in the rain

in the dark

and inspected my terminals

and concluded that

I might need a new battery,

told me to go straight home

and tipped his hat

"Have a nice night."

I see now where Jason gets

his hero complex.

Check Dance

For me, speaking up is like

standing in the open door of

the airplane right before skydiving.

Once I've jumped out, it's not so bad,

but I can't get my feet to leap, to dive.

Our waitress, curly brown hair

pulled away from a face similar to

my mother's with crow's feet and creases

along her cheeks, leaves a single slice of

receipt paper on the tabletop between

Jason and me and my feet hang over

the metal edge of the airplane.

In my head I say

"Hey, excuse me, wait.

Can't you see we are definitely

not together and therefore

need separate checks?"

I swear, Jason ages ten years when he

grabs up the check and reaches into his

back pocket, pulls out a brown leather

wallet with a horse stamped on it, and

he reminds me of a middle-aged guy,

one of those dads, you know,

here, kid, buy yourself something nice,

who is used to paying for the meal.
He might as well take spectacles out of

his breast pocket to calculate the tip.

"I can pay for mine, thanks."

And then he waves me off.

Jason fucking Wells waves me off.

I am quick as a flash. Snatch the bill,

tuck in a twenty, pass it to the waitress

as she slides by with startled eyes,

as close as I'll ever get to skydiving.

Jason's mouth is tilted up in this way that

makes my insides melt like a chocolate bar

on a dashboard in the middle of August.

"Well, this was nice.

Probably time for me to get back."

Closing in on four a.m., but Jason fucking Wells

doesn't even look tired. Mostly, he just looks amused.

He Waits

until we're back outside the 7-11,

standing beside my Volkswagen,

more ancient than Watters,

to say

"So, I'll see you tomorrow night?"

It's the way he says it,

like we've already agreed,

like that's what we were doing

over waffles and black coffee.

"What?

Why?"

Two months is all the time

I have left in Watters.

I'm not here to make friends or allies

or whatever the hell else.

I'm here to pass the hours away

until I have a dorm room

under a different sky

because God knows I can't call Watters home,

not like Jason fucking Wells,

who probably boasts about his hometown

to northerners when he takes trips to

the bright lights of New York City

and pretty girls flirt with him

on the subway because he has

a southern accent and rides horses

and says *howdy*.

Two months is all the time

"Why not?"

There it is again, that question,

but to list all the reasons why

would take the last dregs of this night

and every ounce of strength my throat has left

so instead,

I get in my car

and drive home

without a word.

Part Two

Jason Fucking Wells

Silver Oaks

Mrs. Mackenzie actually does have insomnia

and PTSD from the car accident that made her a widow

and gave her a lifetime of neck spasms

something like a decade before I came into the world.

She told me about it once and then never mentioned it again,

told me that at night she dreams of shattered glass

and a glaring green traffic light, so she sleeps during the day,

assured that eventually a nurse will wake her

from her nightmares.

"Scottish history."

Her voice is a croak like she's smoked since birth

and I lend her a genuine smile, my first in a while,

and stare at the off-color stain on the cushion beside her,

try not to build a list in my brain of its possible origins.

On the cover of Mrs. M's book are rolling Scottish hills

in majestic untouched emerald,

spreading across the glossy front flap.

Mrs. M once told me she wanted to learn everything

before she ran out of time

and I guess what better things are there to do

in the middle of the night than expand your horizons

like a Hollywood vampire whose read everything

Euripides wrote and speaks twenty-seven languages

and is also a master of the violin?

Each night, it's something new by the fireplace that's never lit.

"Aren't you Scottish?"

I am awash with amazement at her triumphant nod,

how proud she can be of a European country she wasn't born in

when I can't even be proud of the soil beneath my feet

with its familiar roads that have raised me.

"Never been there though.

Those Scots, they were a mean folk

but I guess they were all mean

back then."

Mrs. Mackenzie is the grandmother I never had

though I did have one once, a woman named Lucy

on my father's side, until he married my mom

who was, in my grandmother's opinion,

a tramp, a liar, a backwoods hick, or so go the stories

my mother used to tell me back when we actually

talked about things that mattered, and my grandmother

always said I was rude and boyish and not very funny,

and then she died of lung cancer.

"Lots of testosterone in the Highlands, I hear."

Mrs. Makenzie is old but not so old that you feel like

she's slipping away, and she has a crooked back

but she's still sharp as a tack and that's why I love her so much.

She doesn't question my midnight visits

but she sees through them.

It isn't impossible for me to believe that someday,

I will be just like her

except please God, don't let me grow old in Watters.

It Must Have Been My Car

It's conspicuous,

easily recognized by anyone

passing by at night

and glancing into empty parking lots,

an old Volkswagen Golf

painted the color of the sky

on a clear summer day,

with one of those bumper stickers

white and oval-shaped

with a town's initials

you can buy in gift shops

in places like Vegas

and Myrtle Beach,

only I've never been anywhere

so mine says

ANYWHERE BUT HERE.

Hell's Parking Lot

Jason Wells looks unaffected and I decide

that this is what he always looks like,

unaffected, and I sort of want to poke him,

shove him back across the line in the sand

that I keep trying to draw with the tip of my toe

while keeping my distance and affect, affect,

affect him.

"You can't just follow me around town.
It doesn't work that way."

The things I expect include a witty comeback,

the smirk that's haunted me since our first meeting,

a stalker joke, though he doesn't seem the type,

but instead, I get

"You can't just wander around Watters

in the middle of the night.

It doesn't work that way."

But it does work that way. It's worked that way

for almost a year now, for months before Rachel

tied a lasso around my feet, so Jason fucking Wells

should probably mind his own fucking business.

"I fail to see how this is any of your business.

Despite what you and everyone else might think,

you don't actually own this town."

A lie, lie, lie, lie, lie.

"Is that what people think?"

I have never known someone with such

steady eyes, and I'm good at steady,

at standing my ground, lifting my chin,

puffing out my chest, making myself bigger

than my opponent, but Jason is different.

Unaffected. Because he'll always be taller

with square chin and full chest and...

"I'm worried about you."

I feel like someone has pressed pause

on this night. Time-out, wait, hold on a second.

You can't make this stuff up.

Jason Wells, standing outside Silver Oaks,

brown boots against gray concrete, telling a girl

he has known a week that he's worried about her

with puckered brow and sagging shoulders,

and I can't shape my words into anything resembling

a reply, so I get in my car, the slam of the door

like plunging my head underwater, a cocoon of quiet.

The Witching Hour

There are different definitions

just like most things that existed

in the time before meticulous records,

words with meaning after meaning after meaning.

Somewhere between midnight

and three a.m. is the general consensus,

when babies cry and demons creep

and everyone goes home.

The hours in the dead of night

when Jason and I exchange addresses

and meeting times and show up

without a single clue how to define it.

The First Night

The first night I disappeared into the depths of Watters

was not the first night my father came home in a drunken rage.

It was weeks after that first shocking time,

when the very foundation of our home seemed to shift

under the weight of an unexpected fist.

I spent the night at Rachel's, watching movies

and eating junk food and falling asleep just as the clouds

started to turn deep pink low against the horizon

and when I returned home the next morning,

it was to a mother who had no new bruises

but an oddly peaceful veil across her face,

a smoothness to her sleep-flushed epidermis

for the first time since my father's diagnosis.

So the next night, I snuck out my window

seconds after my father stumbled in through the front door

and hid in the bushes at the side of the house, listening.

There was shouting but only shouting.

No sounds of violent outbursts with fists or furniture.

No tear tracks on my mother's skin at breakfast.

It felt like I'd found a key and so I began wandering at night,

starting in my bushes and then behind the wheel of my car

and then gas stations and supermarkets

and the shadows of Watters.

There was no way to know when the key would work

and when it wouldn't, but it was always worth

testing it against the grooves of my father's rage.

Whataburger
Witching Hour #1

I considered a wig, stuffed in a duffel bag,

synthetic Barbie blond tightly secured over

my own mousy mop in the bathroom

or hair dyed over the sink, lollipop purple.

I could paint my car the color of parking lot,

swap the plates with something exotic like Kansas,

rip off the bumper sticker, ball it in my fist,

replace it with MY KID IS AN HONOR STUDENT.

But tonight, I'm not hiding.

I am sitting in a southern burger joint,

a large orange box, every surface coated in a

layer of florescent-lit grease I'm trying not to stare at,

framed in a plate-glass window, on display,

waiting for Jason to come for me

because I know he will.

I skipped dinner so I could eat my weight

in french fries and a triple-meat burger

with all the fixings, and I'm midnight ravenous

when I catch a whiff of beef smothered in ketchup.

And I mean, look, I get that Whataburger has a

theme or whatever and they are sticking to their guns

in an almost shamefully devoted fashion, but when

they had their employee meeting and someone said

"Hey, you know what the theme should be?
Fucking Orange"

he should have been made to stand in the unemployment line

because orange is the worst color that God made, no contest.

I eat my burger, satisfied when a glob of ketchup

slides from the greasy meat and onto the curve of my thumb.

I laugh and think I might be a little hysterical

with the knowledge that I am currently being pursued,

that I can't hide,

like I'm running from Michael Myers, who is walking

because he knows no matter how fast I run,

somehow the fear itself will act as an anchor, and

he'll catch me.

White Trash

Watters is what you might call the sticks

and the people in Watters

are what you might call white trash

or rednecks or hicks.

Jason fucking Wells is not white trash

even though he was born under the same

road signs as Rachel and me and all of Watters High.

Oh no.

People like Jason fucking Wells get to be called cowboys

because even though the redneck stereotype is a description

of his life in his own handwriting—rides a horse,

wears a cowboy hat,

sports a belt buckle the size of a dinner plate,

has a twang, listens to country western music, says

ma'am

and

y'all

and

howdy—

people like Jason fucking Wells will never get called

white trash

because he has money and probably wears tie clips

and only really authentic rodeo belt buckles

when he's out at big fancy meetings

with big fancy ranch owners

just like himself and his father,

and therefore is exempt from insult

even though he lives in this backwoods town

just like the rest of us.

I'm wearing shoes that I got on clearance at the J-Mart on 75,

sitting in a fast food joint, hiding from my alcoholic father who is back at our house that has a screen door with a hole in it.

My car is a hand-me-down that my mom bought on Craigslist

when I was in middle school.

My first job was at the Dairy Queen

on Monroe Street and I had to walk there every day,

showing up with sweat in the pits of my uniform.

I could go on. Really. Forever.

But you get the gist.

So even as the double doors slide on their mechanisms

to admit Jason fucking Wells,

I lean down and lick the ketchup off my hand

in one clean swipe

The Real Tragedy

isn't

that Jason Wells is dressed

not like white trash tonight,

a pair of jeans,

a Honda t-shirt,

a backwards baseball cap

isn't

even that

he doesn't utter a word

as he sits down,

a familiarity

he takes part in

much to my discomfort

is

that as soon as his denim-clad ass

hits the hard-plastic booth,

he reaches across the table

with those hands the size of basketball hoops

and steals one of my french fries.

A Sacrament

The sound I make is not unlike the sputter

that comes from an elephant's trunk

as I snatch my neon orange tray

back against my chest, cover it with my arms,

protect my fried food like a mother

guarding her young from his questing fingers.

"What the fuck?"

I expected unaffected but what I get instead

is something I'm not prepared for: belly laughs.

Jason, head thrown back, throat column exposed,

top row of teeth shining out at me, straight, white, perfect,

while he gasps for breath, his arms outstretched

across the table, bare arms tan and hairy and muscular,

and I'm struck speechless, breathless, completely deceased.

This is not the Jason Wells who stood in a parking lot

twenty-four hours ago and told me he was worried about me.

This guy is young, is my age, is full of red-blooded life.

Sleepy and wholly, disturbingly sexy.

His hand on his stomach, punctuated by a groan.

Mine trembling around my orange tray.

But he just wipes his eyes and says

"If someone had been watching,

they would have thought

I pulled a knife on you."

I try to explain in no uncertain terms

that you can't just eat a girl's Whataburger french fries

because Whataburger french fries are sacred

and explain this around the potatoes in my mouth

while I try to cram in more out of sheer terror

of leaving any behind for him to burgle.

"Here's the Deal

If you want to follow me around Watters every night, that's
fine. I can't stop you, I guess. Free country and all. And seeing
as how you're Jason Wells, I can only assume that even if I tried
to get you to back off, your privilege and general customization
to getting whatever the hell you want would probably lead you
to ignore my wishes like you have thus far, so let's just say that,
for at least the next two weeks, I'm going to be roaming around
Watters from approximately two in the morning to four in the
morning. That's usually about all I need.

Now, assuming that you're just going to find me either way, if
you give me your cell phone number, I would be obliged to let
you know where I'm going to be, you know, to save you the time
and trouble of looking for me. If you show up, the more the
merrier, I suppose, and if not, well maybe you've realized that
my life is boring as fuck and nothing is going on that would
require your tender chaperoning skills or an immediate call to
the Watters press, and that I really am just a waste of time.

You'll also realize that there's no need to worry about my safety because, as I'm sure you know, there hasn't been a murder in Watters since like '82 and that was a domestic thing, so I would probably say that you'll be completely done with this entire circus by the middle of the week. Thursday, if you're really a persistent guy, which I get the feeling you are. Sound okay, Wells?"

His Reply

"I already gave you

my phone number."

I Pretend

not to hear,

ball up my burger wrapper,

the equivalent of going

into a fake tunnel

and hanging up the phone,

and tuck it in my empty

french fry container,

an orange cardboard rectangle

because then I would have to admit

that I threw away that receipt

approximately 3.42 seconds

after he walked out

of Pretzel Mania,

with his flirty smile and

his knowing walk,

strictly out of spite.

But then I decide

to stop pretending.

"Look, Mr. Wells,

you can't just go around

giving girls your number

like a gift and expecting them

to tattoo them on their foreheads.

I threw the damn thing away."

His iPhone makes

a crunchy noise

moving over crumbs

and grease and poorly

administered cleaning solution

to get to me.

"Two one two five"

he says out loud, and the numbers

poke at me like needles.

"You can't just tell me

your lock code."

My voice a hiss,

my eyes darting,

my heart pounding

at the heat of his phone

in my palm,

the weight of it.

"It's not my ATM pin,

for God's sake."

His wallpaper is him

and a horse, jet black.
White trash.

I put my number in,

save it as Bethany,

hesitate, and have

a premonition:

him sending flirty texts

meant for another Bethany

that land in my phone instead,

and an anxious

kind of panic flashes

behind my eyes

like someone has threatened

my very life,

prickling heat all down

my back and arms.

In his contacts,

I quickly—subtly, I think—

check for another Bethany,

but there is only

a Cassie, an Emily,

a Jessie, a Molly.

I shut off the screen,

slide the phone back to him,

guilty as fuck.

Jason looks, you guessed it,

unaffected, but knowing,

and it's the knowing

that scares me.

"Deal?"

I count the seconds:

thirty, forty, one hundred thirty-two,

before he answers.

"Deal."

Keeping Secrets

"So, what have you been up to?"

Sometimes I think Rachel can read my mind.

My stomach will rumble for pizza, a craving in my tastebuds,

and she will invite me over for a stuffed-crust pie

with mushrooms and spinach, without my ever saying a word.

She can tell, even from four states away,

that I'm keeping something close to my chest,

something I feel the need to grip in both fists,

since I can't find a way to put words to it.

"Nothing.
Working."

When Rachel returns home,

stuffing herself back into the box that is Watters,

I'll tell her about Jason, the story that will have

reached its final pages by the time she crosses state lines.

"Man, you sure are boring without me."

Truer words

were never spoken.

The History of Rachel and Bethany

Rachel and I have been two seeds

sprouting in the same soil since before we could talk.

There are only so many daycares,

so many elementary schools, in a small town like Watters,

lined up on Monroe Street like the Palace Guard,

and like something written in the stars,

it was always the two of us with desks side-by-side

and our own lunch table and color-coordinated prom dresses.

We shot up together, ivy growing up the wall,

through our awkward middle school years,

heartbreaking crushes, nights spent

pasting science projects to tri-folds.

We never meant to keep everyone else at a distance

but the two of us were our own ecosystem,

sheltered in our bubble, a habitat we nurtured only for us.

I once prayed the prayer of a hopeful child

that I could be just like her

or that we could somehow merge into a single being.

Even before the violence began, she seemed to understand

some secret about existing in the world without

the need to hide, without the need to survive in the dark.

Rachel has always been a flower turned up to the sun,

while I am a root, buried, stuck, trapped in the dirt.

Purple Raincloud
Witching Hour #2

I choose the head shop on 35 in a bizarre attempt

to derail our bizarre deal because Jason Wells

seems like he might be the kind of guy

to shake his head at pot-smoking,

one of those cute country boys who goes to church on Sunday

and doesn't believe in committing most sins

with the exception of having sex with their girlfriends

which is okay until someone gets pregnant.

But if Jason fucking Wells has a problem with head shops,

he doesn't seem to have a problem with this one

because he strolls the shelves like he's out for a browse

at a Whole Foods Market on a Sunday afternoon.

Louis, named after the King of France, and I

lean into the counter from opposite sides

over pipes and bongs locked behind glass,

watch Jason like he's a crocodile slipping through a lake.

"What the hell is Sheriff Woody

doing in my shop?"

One lifted eyebrow, a multicolored hook through it

with a spike on each end that I helped him pick out

from the jewelry department of J-Mart,

that ring and two others on sale for less than five dollars.

"Do I need to call the cops?"

Opposites

I started coming to the head shop

back when I was dating Louis

almost a year ago, when Dad

first started to drink for real

and Watters became my escape

and the thing I needed to escape

and even though I knew I wasn't

in love with Louis, I liked him enough

and he didn't really want to hang out

unless he could call me his girlfriend

and I was mostly okay with it

because even though he smokes pot

and cigarettes and probably other things,

he always smells like Old Spice

and tastes like spearmint gum

so it wasn't like it was a sacrifice

to kiss him for hours in this shop

and stick my hands under his beanie

and into his hair, all dark and curled,

and when he worked overnight shifts

like he is right now, I liked to come and

sit behind the counter with him

and play his old Gameboy Color.

Jason Wells is whatever Louis isn't.

He is put-together and looks like

he knows his concrete opinion on any subject,

which is a speed I can't keep up with,

in a way that says he's always quietly thinking

even if he doesn't say much out loud.

Calamity

I'm staring at Jason

and he's also staring back

and when the hell did I

stop looking at bongs?

And then I jerk away bodily

and knock over an ash tray,

a painfully red glass strawberry,

and watch it fall in slow motion

until it shatters into about

three thousand pieces against

the hard, concrete flooring

at my feet, like a bloody curse.

"Fuck."

Jason is already on the floor,

reaching down to pick up

ceramic shards, cradled

in the palm of his overly large

hand, and against his tan skin,

between his life lines and

callouses, the broken pieces

look like poppy petals.

"Sorry about that."

My mouth should be the exit

for those words, but it's Jason

that says them, the fragments

of the ash tray sprinkling the counter

and then a twenty-dollar bill

fluttering down to cover them

like a peace offering, a white flag,

an apology that isn't his to make

and then Louis shatters the silence.

"Dude,

are you for real?"

Angry

When I was little, my mother used to say

that I could never hide my anger

because it turned me into a cherry,

a strawberry, a tomato.

The flush, the rage that always somehow

started in my throat and spread

to the back of my neck, the tips of my ears,

the expanse of my cheeks,

like fields catching on fire.

My skin gave me away

every time.

Wait

"Bethany.

Come on, Bethany.

Wait."

Oh.

He wants me to wait.

Fuck him.

Hell's Parking Lot Part II

I see the hardened ridge of Jason's biceps

even in the inky darkness of the parking lot,

no street lamps, against my own useless effort

to bring my car door closed, and it's no use

because this guy moves hay bales and

tractor wheels for a living, wrangles with horses,

handles rope like it's shoestring, so I stop trying,

the fight going out of me like an exorcism of my insides.

"What did I do wrong?"

And maybe that's the worst part: that he doesn't know,

that he can't even comprehend how what he did

might be offensive, might be embarrassing

and I shouldn't have to educate him, but I know I will.

"You can't just whip your wallet out

and think that makes you a good person.

I should have been the one to pay for it.

You can't just make people like you

by paying for everything."

Pity

Honestly, I don't mean half of what I said. I don't think Jason pays for things to make people like him. I don't even think he pays for things because he maybe knows I'm struggling, that my family has a fraction of the money that his family is sure to have. Nobody is creeping on my lawn at night to see if I have an observatory.

I think he pays for things because he can and because he thinks it's nice and maybe because his father taught him that's what gentlemen do

and maybe if I was someone else, it would be totally okay but I'm not someone else. I'm me, poor me, whose parents can't afford to help her pay for car insurance or gas, much less the complete and utter hell of college tuition and so when he does shit like this, it just feels like he's taking pity on me, like he feels like he needs to pay because he can, like he's *saying it's okay, sweetheart, I've got this*

and oh God, I fucking hate that so much.

"I didn't mean to upset you."

The way his voice c r a c k s with sincerity is the worst. He is no longer unaffected. No. He's very affected.

"It's okay. Just… stop paying for things."

And I suppose, in some weird way, this is enough for both of us to feel content that we still are whatever we thought we were before this calamity.

J-Mart
Witching Hour #3

is the place where people in Watters

go when they're looking for laundry detergent

and corn chips in the middle of the night,

where I have spent more time under

the cover of night than I have ever spent

while the sun was still shining,

roaming toy aisles, shopping for children

that don't exist, and pharmacy aisles

for fake people with fake ailments.

I pass people looking sleepy with half gallons

of milk in their hands and fleece pajama bottoms,

lined up like this is the premiere event

and maybe it is because the line is so long

it's curving a little to the left, scooping around

a display of Fourth of July decorations.

Tastes

For me, it always comes back to the food.

I have a love affair with tastes.

I calculate the cost of a box of cherry Pop-Tarts

against the cash in my pocket, half the price

of the real cherries Jason chose without looking at the cost.

"How do you survive on a diet like that?"

I can only assume this insulting question is in reference

to the Pop-Tarts and the Pringles and the store-brand

creamy peanut butter I'm holding in my arms like new life.

Or perhaps it's in reference to the loaf of white bread

I have curled in my hand, the cheap kind that costs less

than a dollar and is probably just cotton candy.

My peanut butter baby is slipping out of the crook of my elbow

and Jason scoops in like someone I'm meant to pass the ball to,

begins unloading my armful,

which to him is only half an armful.

My weak protests, things like

"I've got it"

fall on chivalrous ears because I've already activated

his Boy Scout mode, only deactivated by a full reboot,

and who's got the time?

We give up and get a cart, a navy-blue atrocity with

a squeaky wheel, a discarded produce bag in the child's seat.

He picks out peppers, red ones, with a pensive focus

I have only seen used while trying to parallel park.

I don't know the first thing about picking out peppers,

other than you don't buy the ones that have started to rot,

but I plunge my hand into the bin to feel the soft, leathery skin

against my fingers and pull it back out to smell

the bitter pepper scent that sticks to my palms,

and I feel Jason's eyes like heat.

I watch him right back, picking out organic mushrooms

and then bananas, corn, celery, zucchini, grapefruit.

The starting line: Aisle 3, right after the frozen foods,

sharing cart space, food mingling, like this is okay.

His can of tomato soup rolls against my box of

Lucky Charms then stops and rolls back.

When I toss in a box of bowtie pasta, it lands on top

of his bag of veggie chips with a crackling crunch.

My jar of pasta sauce sits next to his bottle of 3-in-1

shampoo in companionable silence.

"How can shampoo be 3-in-1?

What 3 things do you even put in your hair?"

He counts them off on his fingers: shampoo,

conditioner, body wash.

"You combine your shampoo and your body wash?"

We stand in line, now shaped like a J, munching

on his organic strawberries, dance around each other

for who can be the first to pile their food on the belt,

and I am caught, incapacitated, by the shade of his mouth,

bright red with strawberry juice.

Life in the Daytime

Breakfast with Mom before

I move sleepily to the strip mall,

where salted pretzels await me

for a six-to-eight-hour shift

that ends in the taste of pepperoni

or garlic or cinnamon on my lips

that I take home with me to the quiet hours

when both of my parents are still

floating through their own half-lives.

Before graduation changed things,

these were the quiet hours I craved,

full of homework and reality TV,

but now, they are the vacant hours

I spend trying not to think,

trying to drown out the sound

of boot heels on linoleum

and Jason's deep laugh,

trying to undo the things knotting in me

when I remember the sound

of him biting into a fresh strawberry.

Mom always comes home first

and we eat dinner together,

usually something I make from a box

while she curls into herself at

the table, exhausted from her long day

at work, but preparing for a long night

at home, and then we go our separate ways

again, her to the couch where she will

watch the news or medical dramas

while I sit in my room, but we are together

in disconnected spaces, waiting, waiting,

her for the monster who will appear

and me for two a.m., when I will slip

out my window and be gone.

Waffle House
Witching Hour #4

"Now I'm starting to think

you just wander around at night

so you can eat in peace."

A river of ketchup drowns my hashbrowns,

floating into a moat around the dark,

crunchy potatoes, Jason a blur beyond them.

"If I wanted peace,

I wouldn't have given you

my phone number."

Trying to hide a smile behind a laminated menu

only works when you don't have the kind of smile

that spreads all the way up to

the pupils of your eyes.

"Don't know if you noticed

but there aren't a whole lot of places

to go this late at night.

It's Watters, for God's sake.

Nobody is awake after nine unless

they're serving coffee to the likes of us."

Crossed arms, those biceps

as distracting as the sun right in your eye

while you're driving straight toward it.

And I sense it like the tickle of a sneeze

in the back of your throat, from the twist

of his mouth and the scrutiny in his eyes.

Jason has never had smothered hashbrowns

and he has already passed judgement when

they've never had the chance to pass his lips.

Believer

Jason Wells has the face of a five-year-old

who is convinced they're allergic to broccoli

because of the adult color and steamed scent

without ever having tasted it, a borderline fear

of perhaps unfamiliarity or just disappointment.

His examination of the plate I ordered him,

hashbrowns covered in onions and peppers,

tiptoes on dubious investigation as if he will discover,

if he squints just hard enough, that the contents

of the plate are actually slithering in his direction.

The ketchup bottle, oblong and cold under the

AC vent that's fluttering our napkins, held down

by slightly smudged, overused and over-washed

silverware, stands watch, my fingertips inching it

until Jason's sneer makes me grab it back, poor thing.

I almost combust, holding in my cutting comments

as he cuts into the hot fried potatoes with the enthusiasm

of a medical examiner cutting into a fresh corpse

and crunches the bite between his teeth, has to crunch

because I always order them cooked that way.

When Jason swallows, his Adam's apple bobbing in

an entirely distracting dip of a pattern, he has turned

into a pillar, Lot's wife in salt granules across the table,

unmoving, unspeaking, no longer unaffected, and the word

he finally utters, exalting in its singularity and bite.

"Fuck."

Be Careful

I can't say when my mother

first decided to remain silent.

Maybe it was after the diagnosis

or when the first bruises started

to blossom on her arms

and she discovered that keeping

her jaw clenched was easier

than having it broken.

We were never the mother-daughter pair

who giggled over boys and formals,

but there was a time at least

when she wasn't a statue,

when our house wasn't a mausoleum

where we spoke only in whispers.

Mom made spaghetti and curry

and chicken and dumplings,

had laugh lines around her eyes

and a signature lipstick.

I remember her in color

but now she's black and white

in the glow of the refrigerator,

telling me she'll heat up leftovers

if I'm hungry.

"You need to be quieter

when you come in.

You woke your father last night

closing the door."

My mother speaking so calmly

about my reappearance from the

depths of middle-of-the-night Watters

is like finding out your biology teacher

has a first name, a spouse, a house on your block.

"Did he...?"

I noticed no new bruises today

but I find myself more and more negligent,

staying out later and forgetting to check

when I come back home for broken things

and broken bones, forget to watch

my mother from behind my hand, to look

for black eyes and split lips.

"Everything's fine. Just be careful."

Those words have become a dismissal,

a way to say goodbye or have a nice day

in the murky quiet of a cemetery after dark.

Step lightly, keep your voice down, be careful.

Fraser Park
Witching Hour #5

The heavy, tangible need to see

Jason Wells try all the best things

I can offer him is the only thing

that could coerce me to pack a lunch

and by pack a lunch, I, of course, mean

I stole my stash from my closet and

the one in my backpack and the one in my car,

shrink-wrapped goods tucked away

in the depths of an old paper sack, now

sitting between Jason and me on the lip

of the fountain, still a little hot from the sun.

"Did you hold up the gas station

or something?"

Twinkies, Pringles, teriyaki beef jerky,

Cheeto Puffs, Honey Buns, cake balls,

Swedish Fish, peach salsa

and yellow corn chips with lime salt on them.

"The fact that you had never had Waffle House hashbrowns

disturbed me greatly so I'm going to need you to point

to anything you've never had so you can try it immediately."

I watch the path of his hand, gritting back a shiver

at the way his fingertips graze everything,

goosebumps racing along the surface of my skin

as if he's touched me directly.

"You've never had TWINKIES?

I can't be seen with someone

who's never eaten a Twinkie."

Jason gestures with hand, wrist, bicep,

shoulder, as if to say, *who's going to see us?*

but that's not the point.

Tastes Part II

It's not that I don't like healthy things.

I like vegetables as much as the next person,

the solid, washed-out flavor of brussels sprouts

or the tight crunch of finger-length carrots,

but given the choice between broccoli and

brownies, well, that's no choice at all.

We eat Swedish Fish, staining our lips red,

and the peach salsa, parted and scooped

by chips that leave salt on our fingers,

and then the cake balls: double chocolate

with sea salt, big and square like pastry sprinkles

and he gets that look on his face like he did

when he ate the hashbrowns, before his lips

come around his teeth and he takes a deep breath

like he needs the comfort of extra oxygen

and I didn't realize until just now that the

helpless look on his face is why I'm sitting

in a sea of wrappers and sugar crumbs,

that I needed the assurance somehow

that long after these nights are over,

long after I've become a speck in his memory,

he'll remember that I was the one to show him

how to appreciate something sweet on his tongue

but he's moved on to the Twinkies while

I've been distracted with some kind of rushed

excitement that fizzes in my blood

and the look on his face is close to orgasmic

and I am too fragile for this—

cracked open like a nesting doll, all my smaller

selves spilling out in front of me, selves

that are softer, vulnerable, susceptible, delicate,

so I avert my eyes, resist the urge to plug my ears

when he groans even as I refuse to give purchase

to the part of me who is desperate to know

how sweet his mouth tastes.

Pretzel Mania Part II

We're not supposed to see each other

in the light of day, an agreement I realize now

I've only made with him inside my head,

but it's nevertheless rather jarring when

the next day, while the sun is shining bright

and there are actually people awake

and moving around on the surface of the Earth,

Jason walks into Pretzel Mania.

"I've made a decision"

he says against the glass of the display case

before choosing a pepperoni pretzel with the

tip of his index finger and not his words

because his mouth is too busy saying things like

"I know this is *your* thing"

and

"I don't want to get in your way but..."

Watching his pretzel turn brown in the oven,

which isn't even something I have to do

but there's no one else in line, so screw it—

and if you're going to eat a pepperoni pretzel

it should be a warm and gooey one—

is easier than watching him take up all the room

in the shop, and when the marinara sauce

inside the pretzel begins to ooze, I take it out,

press it into slick parchment paper.

He hands me a slip of paper, like currency

for his oven-hot pretzel, an address written on it

in shockingly messy handwriting because

I guess I thought that everything about Jason

would be perfect, put-together, immaculate,

but now I know that everything about Jason

is just surprising instead.

"Meet me there tonight.

Let me choose for a little while."

A little while. Does he even realize that I'm

interpreting his words like an archeologist with

a brush, eyes eating up ancient symbols carved

into rock and trying to read a foreign timeline?

"You came all the way here

just to bring me this?

You have my phone number."

He folds back a waxy paper corner and exposes

his pretzel to the steamy air, presses a bite

to the dense bread, the marinara sauce seeping

from one side and coating his upper lip, and

I am enthralled as his tongue snakes out to get it.

"But a text message

wouldn't come with a pizza pretzel."

I have created a monster.

"Does this mystery locale have food?"

Two girls that I recognize from Watters High—

freshmen last year—squeeze in behind Jason.

The lobby of Pretzel Mania is about as spacious

as a twin-sized bed with four people in it,

and I expect Jason to vacate the premises to make room,

as he takes up twice as much space as twice

the average human, but instead, he compresses

himself into the microscopic space between the

fountain drink stand and the afternoon-bright window,

almost knocking down a sign for BOGO parmesan pretzels.

The rest of us, these two girls and me,

squished into this vestibule with him, watch,

and like a fish in an aquarium, he has no idea that he's

the center of attention, floating in his own world,

as he goes to town on his pepperoni pretzel.

The girls blush, whisper, giggle.

The Legacy of Jason Wells

Everybody in Watters

who is prone to crushes on boys

has a crush on Jason Wells.

That's just how it is.

Whether they've met him

or not.

Even if their crush is actually

on a story they once heard,

a figure they saw in a field

as they drove past Wells Ranch,

the feel of living in a town

that can somehow boast celebrity.

I see him just like everyone else does,

fixing the fence that lines Monroe Street

on my way to work.

I hear the stories about how he once

saved a ranch hand from being trampled,

helped deliver a breeched foal,

sat by his mother's side

as she slowly faded from cancer.

I am not impervious

to the legacy

of Jason Wells.

24-Hour Chapel
Witching Hour #6

Jason brings food and

even though there's no sign,

no explicit foreboding,

food feels unwelcome here.

Coming here at night

feels like a dream where

something is just off enough

to tip you off that it's a dream—

a room the wrong color,

your mother with longer hair,

your bedroom on the wrong

side of the house.

The chapel is petite.

Four tiny pews and loud

hardwood under my feet,

a cross at the front with bibles

at its foot, a prayer box,

paper, pens.

"What are we doing here?"

He extends a Dallas Cowboys

lunch box, for crying out loud,

and I open it with a

rapidly sinking heart

to find baby carrots, grapes,

celery, fresh spinach,

just leaves sitting alone,

and who eats just raw spinach?

"Praying, I guess."

We're in a twenty-four-hour chapel

the size of a closet on a dirt road

far north of Watters, in front of

a Presbyterian church off exit 19.

I would never have ventured this far

on my own, not even if it meant

more interesting places.

The places in Watters are interesting

enough when you're a girl,

alone at night.

I didn't know a silence like this

existed, a silence so complete

that it is a tangible presence,

like something sneaking up

behind you, and I reach for

a baby carrot, just to break it

with the crunch of my teeth

in this vegetable.

And then,

another sound.

Jason's Truth

"I started coming here as soon as I got a driver's license. Well, I guess that's not really true. I started coming here when I got my permit because, well... I don't get pulled over, like, ever.

I took off one night right after my mom died. My horse threw me, and I freaked out. It's a weird thing, I guess, to feel like you've been betrayed by an animal, but that's how I felt. My once source of comfort, gone in a second.

So I took off. I don't even know where I was going. I was just going to get on the highway and drive until I was somewhere else. I had money, and it wasn't like my dad was going to come find me.

That's the thing about my dad: to him, I've always been an adult, ever since I could talk. Why should he chase after me if I chose to go?

I ran out of gas right on the highway, under the sign for exit 19, and I found this place on my way to a gas station, and I started coming here every night.

Because, you see, I really do have insomnia. I didn't used to, but after Mom died, Dad started pacing the house, and I couldn't get any sleep, so I started staying up instead.

Anyway, I haven't been here since you climbed the side of my house..."

Attraction

While I lay in bed with Jason's voice

ringing in my ears, the shape of his story

behind my eyelids, watching the sky turn bright

at the curve of the world, I know

the way you know you're getting the flu,

the way you know someone is standing behind you,

the way you know that something bad has happened

when your phone rings late at night. I know

I like Jason fucking Wells, like the way he whispered

his secrets to me as if we were in a crowded room

but he only wanted me to hear, the way he munched

away on celery and, yes, dry fucking spinach after he told me.

But this wasn't in the plan. To drive him crazy,

get rid of him, make him regret ever noticing me

in the first place—that was the plan.

Not to like him,

to feel sympathy for him,

to understand him,

to know him.

The Cyclops
Witching Hour #7

Silence is a word this place has never uttered

in bells and voices and pop music.

In lights that flash blue and green like the

the inside of a cotton candy tube

and it is bizarre how we're not the only ones,

like the population of Oklahoma is not in fact

at home in their beds but right here in Oklahoma City

exactly three point eight miles outside of the

zagged square lines of Bay County.

Jason brought snacks again: tiny grape tomatoes

and sugar snap peas that have been baked in olive oil

and are obviously masquerading as chips.

I ignore his food and buy a pizza big enough for both

our appetites and we eat it and watch a couple

murder zombies with plastic handguns.

Our silence, drowned in chaotic noise

tells me that maybe he can feel, the way I can,

that something is different, that something has shifted,

the way I keep my eyes on the swirling lights

because my gaze wants to linger over him,

face bathed in pink neon, over how his fingers

slide over the skin of a tomato held in his palm,

so subtle, like a caress that makes me shiver.

We climb into the Star Trek game, a black

plastic box in the center of the arcade with a

bucket seat and a screen the size of my windshield.

It's a cave but loud, the lights like flash bangs

as we shoot at Borg soldiers, watch them collapse

and crack up because the game is so 90s

but then we both die and we're left panting

in the dark that's closing in around us,

like it's pressing us—already sitting so close

that our hips are touching—toward each other

and I scramble out of the game, try to

slow the sprint of my heartbeat, the tremble in

my knuckles as we stand in the parking lot,

alone, just us two, counting the seconds until

I can garble a goodbye and jump in my getaway car.

The Truth About Thunderstorms

When I was a little kid,

I was afraid of thunderstorms.

When the thunder would start

and I wished I could be with my mother,

I would hide in my closet instead.

My father always said that big girls

didn't sleep with their parents

and even though I knew my mother

wanted to protest, she never did

so I would hide in my closet

with my knees pulled up to my chest,

hoping that I could escape it,

the heavy drum and cymbal sounds

of the rattling thunder.

You see, I thought that every storm

meant a tornado, and that just like in

The Wizard of Oz, a tornado was going to

sweep up my house and land me somewhere else.

Only, I knew it didn't work that way

because in Oklahoma, they teach you in school

what to do in case of a tornado,

about how you should move to a central room,

away from windows, and cover your head and pray

because if you get sucked out by a tornado,

it can drop you clear across town, and while

the tornado rarely kills you, the drop will every time.

Possibility
Witching Hour #8

This is what I do now when I hear my father's voice

boom loud as thunder: I go to my closet, and I

pull my knees up to my chest

and I squeeze my eyes shut, and I pray.

But there are no sirens tonight, no warning

before the east wind that crashes in, all veins

and high blood pressure and purple cheeks

and I get a lesson in just how much I've miscalculated

because my father is not oblivious to my

I will now make this girl disappear act,

only good at ignoring it, one less person in his way.

But according to him, three days ago,

someone saw Jason and me alone

together in Fraser Park, at night,

a spot notorious for parking lot hookups

and he could not stand the idea that his daughter,

who he barely knows exists in the world,

might be doing something to embarrass him

and he has been waiting, stalking his prey,

for a moment when my car is still in the driveway,

coming home half an hour early to confront me.

And by God, he's confronting me now

with his hands wrapped so tight around my upper arms

and I know there will be bruises

because there are always bruises.

"WHAT THE HELL HAVE YOU

BEEN DOING EVERY NIGHT?

OUT THERE GIVING IT TO SOME BOY?

YOU SLUT."

The first time my father spoke to me like this,

it wasn't the words that left the imprint of nightmares

in my cells or the way his hand snaked out so fast,

before I could even react, to leave a palm print on my cheek.

It was the monster who had snuck in, wearing

the face of my father, who's always liked his liquor,

getting tipsy on craft beer and masculine cocktails

while watching football games and over dinner at Applebee's.
Nothing serious, nothing dangerous, some harmless fun.

And so, that first time, I didn't know

to be scared, to be careful, to tip toe.

I know better now not to flinch when he calls me a slut,

a word he's never used in my presence before tonight,

especially not referring to me,

and I know that any answer I give will be the wrong answer

and I would rather be punished for no answer at all

than for the truth that doesn't belong to him

so I keep my mouth shut, and I learn my lesson

while my mother screams from the hallway.

I imagine that I am back in that chapel with Jason,

in the silence, just the whisper of breath in the quiet air.

Somewhere, Jason is waiting for me at an address

he texted me hours ago, trailed with a smiley face,

and even though last night was something like a disaster

of multicolored lights and pitch-black arcade corners

excitement has been awake inside me all day,

twisting and turning in my stomach, all the blood

puddling and tingling in my fingertips because

there has been a cloud of possibility

hanging blissfully heavy over me, all around me,

since we parted in the parking lot near dawn

but I can feel that cloud raining down on me now,

pelting me with a torrent that leaves pink welts

for acting a fool, letting my guard down,

for hoping for even a moment that something good

could be mine.

The Cemetery

The Watters Cemetery sits on a dirt road

that peters out to nothing but open fields,

no reason to even drive by unless you were

on your way to visit the dead or to get lost

but the cemetery is substantial,

with mausoleums and angel statues,

park benches and flowers at some of the graves

that are fresh, not even wilted in the summer heat.

My butt is parked in the grass beside

a black metal bench because sitting on it

feels wrong when I have no relatives

or friends under any of these headstones

and I don't know if I'm trespassing,

if the ghosts inside these coffins have

business hours, or if I will eventually sink

into the soft dirt under me, but I don't care.

Searching

When he finally comes,

like I knew he would,

I'm turned away from him,

my face hidden by the shadows

and the darkness and my hair

so he can't see the damage,

but his voice is laced with panic,

a quake under his confidence, anyway.

"God, Bethany.

I've been looking all over for you.

Why didn't you meet me?

Why didn't you tell me where you were?"

Because

Because we're not friends,

I want to say.

Because I have no obligation to you,

I want to say.

Because I should be able to do something like this alone,

I want to say.

Because I don't want to need you,

I want to say.

Skin

Jason slides off the park bench,

a slice of sun-warm putty,

down into the grass

but I still won't turn to him.

His radiator-warm hand

that smells like sweat

in the best way

conforms to my jaw.

His thumb burrows

into the dip of my chin,

pulling like he already knows

what he's going to find

on my skin.

His eyes take stock

of my face, a bruise

on the bend of my cheekbone,

a tire-tread pattern of

broken skin mingling

with the hairs of my eyebrow,

a blooming discoloration

on the severe cliff of my jaw.

Jason is unmovable

on a good day

and solid as a brick wall

when he means it, but

his hands are concrete

split open by tremors,

fingertips quivering

across the planes of my skin.

Spill

"My father was diagnosed with a brain tumor almost exactly a year ago. Before that, he was, let's say, difficult. Short temper, broken things here and there, nothing serious, certainly nothing threatening to Mom or me.

But after the diagnosis, he got angry, really angry. That's when he started drinking, more than average, more than above average, so far past above average that he lost his job, where he made money and felt important and bossed people around in the right setting, and had to take a new one he felt was beneath him, and now just spends his time drinking, moping, being angry.

Dying.

Mom works an ungodly amount to make up for my father's lack of income. He doesn't even seem to understand that when he dies, which will probably be rather soon, that she'll be alone with the bills and the mortgage and me.

At least there are no hospital bills because he's refusing to be treated, refusing anything stronger than what he can get in an orange bottle.

My dad's always been an enigma: mysterious past, odd emotional responses, that sort of thing, but I never would have pegged him for cruelty. What he does to Mom, the way he destroys her, that's cruel.

When he goes, she'll be stuck with his debt and his empty liquor bottles and the stench of him all over the house that she'll probably have to sell just to keep her head above water.

I stay out at night to avoid my dad, to make sure he doesn't have a chance to do what he did tonight. My mistake. I've just been holding on until I can get out, until I can escape, until I can get away from Watters and away from him."

Wells Ranch Part II

I don't know what I'm doing here in the kitchen

of Wells Ranch, drinking Earl Grey tea,

which makes me feel like I should be smoking a pipe

and wearing one of those jackets with the elbow patches.

Jason is staring at me, and it would be unsettling

if I didn't find his hulking presence so comforting.

"He thinks I sneak out every night

to meet a boy, and he's right."

The world goes hazy around the edges when he

traces his thumb along the dried blood in my eyebrow

so slowly I think I can make out the ridges of his fingerprint, not enough to keep me from gritting my teeth.

That one hurt the worst by far. The other bruises

on my cheek, my jaw, came from Dad's fist,

the blows lessened just barely by Jack Daniels

and my mother attempting to stay his hand,

but the one on my eyebrow is the handiwork of the edge

of my bedside table, when he threw me with such force,

I saw black when I collided with the furniture,

and he screamed that if I got pregnant,

he would force me to get rid of it.

It throbs and burns and aches, the swell of it hot and sore.

Jason presses two brownish orange ibuprofen pills

into my palm which I toss back immediately

and wash down with the tea that scalds the roof

of my mouth in a wave of steaming bergamot.

"You can't go back there."

That's What They All Say

It's what Rachel said.

It's what Louis said.

It's what Jason is saying.

But none of them get it.

I don't have anywhere else to go.

"I Wish This Never Happened to You"

he says.

This gives me pause.

It's the first time someone has

said it in just this way.

Such a simple thing

but not simple at all.

It's not a wish for it to stop

but a wish for it have never happened

in the first place.

The Question

"Where will you go

at the end of the summer?"

The Answer

"Somewhere that's not here."

But Really

"Colorado.

In a little

over a month."

And while the sad crease

of his eyes

and mouth

don't surprise me.

The sad crease of mine

does.

Thor

Rachel has had an affection for horses

since we saw Black Beauty in third grade,

collecting stuffed ponies and horse figurines

and books on stallions

but I've always been a little wary of anything

that could stamp me out of existence without effort

but Jason insists that if I meet Thor, I'll feel better,

as if it will be comforting to meet yet another man

who could kill me.

Thor is an ungodly huge creature and even though

I just told Jason I'm not scared of horses exactly,

I'm a little scared of this one, looming over me

like a shadow in a nightmare and looking down

with dark, glossy horizontal eyes that assure me of

their ability to kill.

"Hey, it's okay.

He just wants to say hi."

He must know the look of his own menace

because he hangs his head over the stall door,

looking up under the thick lashes of his wet eyes

like a child trying to prove their innocence

and with Jason's safe heat behind me,

his eyes look more like melting chocolate than

the unknown color of death.

"Hi."

His muzzle feels like crushed velvet soaked in water,

his hair dry and stringy but in a pleasant way,

as I learn the feel of him and the smell of him

and I'm adrift for the seconds it takes for him to

grow bored of me.

"He likes you."

There is something about the tone of his words,

the feel of it as it rumbles through my back

where he has somehow become pressed to me,

that makes me dissolve like sugar in warm water,

makes me wonder if there is another message

floating in the undercurrent.

At the Door

This is the part that I always replay in my mind,

the way that Jason Wells walks me to the door

as the sun is starting to make its grand entrance.

I know that he's tired, can see it in the way his

eyelids droop and how he walks even slower

than usual, a saunter, an amble.

But when we get there, standing toe-to-toe,

he pushes the tips of his fingers in little circles

around the bruises on my face like he's trying

to make sure they stay contained to the purple

areas that they've already marred

and then the very tip of his index finger

traces my chin in the softest touch

that anyone has ever lain against my skin

and I have to step back quick

because I feel like there's a storm brewing inside me,

something tumultuous and chaotic.

I thank him for the tea, for the ibuprofen, for just

generally being an excellent human being,

and then I'm out the door and in my car.

One More Thing

But when the door closes and my headlights

push up against it like a flood trying to get in,

I am motionless, like my limbs are underwater.

I tell myself to put the car in drive, to pull around

in their U-shaped driveway and out onto Monroe Street,

toward home and my father, who by now is already passed out,

but I don't.
Instead,
I get out.

I mingle with my golden headlights, moving so slow,

like trying to run in a dream, and press my knuckles

against his door but never get the chance to knock.

Jason opens it so fast that I wonder if he ever left it at all

or if he was watching from the window as I decided to

come back, decided just one more thing.

"I just...

I just wanted to..."

I push up on my toes, all the way up to him,

miles and miles away, press my hand to the back

of his always sun-hot neck so I don't miss.

The Kiss

Warm

arms going around me,

breath puffing against my lips,

tongue searching for mine,

air coming in through the open door,

blaze of my headlights flooding us,

hands pressing me to the doorjamb.

Long enough

for his fingers to find a good grip on my hip,

for my hands to find their way into his hair,

for every part of me to start throbbing,

like the throb in my eyebrow but somewhere

in the neighborhood of my zipper.

Want

is something I know well,

in pictures of far-off places and

the smell of baking bread hanging in the air

and the taste of freedom on the tip of my tongue

but I have never known it quite like this.

Part Three
Burning

A Figure Study of My Mother

She's sitting at the kitchen table

with a coffee mug cupped in her hands

and a gash on her lip,

eyes vacant in that way

that says she's trying not to see anything,

the gaze of the dead,

bruised elbow bent against the table,

against the pain,

feet crossed at the ankles

to appear unperturbed,

but the porcelain white

of her cheeks speaks louder

of sleepless nights

and agitated conversations

and fear buried deep,

her skin purple around the edges,

blue with veins

and bruises

and melancholy.

In Which Rachel Sees
Right Through Me

I'm helping Rachel hang up her clean clothes

when she gets back from California

because that's what best friends do, I suppose.

"If you wash them at the hotel before you pack them

then when you get home,

all you have to do is put them away.

It's miraculous."

I want to tell her that the true definition

of miraculous is Jason Wells' mouth

and the thick press of him through his jeans.

"You're quiet."

I blink down at Mickey Mouse's wrinkled face,

clenched in my sweaty fists that were imagining

being clenched in Jason's hair.

"Just a lot on my mind.

I should probably get home actually."

Rachel blocks the doorway

before I can run.

"Like I Don't Know

Oh honey, if you think you're getting out that easily, you are sorely mistaken. Not only do you have to explain what those cuts and bruises are because, of course, I noticed them even though you obviously tried to cover them up with make-up which, just so you know, didn't work even a little bit, but you also have to explain why you're so damn jumpy so you better spill."

Choices

She lets me choose

the order of information,

the specific chronological way

that I hand her the facts,

the non-linear spillage

of last night's events

because the bruises

should come first,

like they did

on the timeline,

but she lets me start

with Jason.

How to Tell Your Best
Friend You Made Out
With Jason Wells

You stutter

and stop for long

silent periods,

trying to word things

in the exact right way.

You do everything

to avoid eyes

because dear Lord

her eyes see right

through you

every time

and you know

what she's going to say,

of course you do,

so you just blurt

"I've been hanging out with Jason Wells

and I kissed him last night."

Told You So

She doesn't say it

but she doesn't say it

in that way that tells me

specifically that she's

not saying it because

she knows I already know

that she has every right

to say it and so

she doesn't say it

but it's written

all over her face.

"He's nice and cute

and he has a horse

named Thor."

Her sandy yellow eyebrows

merge with her hairline

and she is shocked sunshine.

"You met his horse?"

The way she says it

almost sounds dirty

like horse is a euphemism

and I feel the flush start

in the shells of my ears.

There were definitely no

euphemistic horse meetings

in Jason's doorway

last night.

"Have you told him that

when you go to Colorado,

you're not coming back?"

Reasons Why I Haven't Told Jason I'm Not Coming Back

1. He didn't ask.

2. It's not something you just blurt out.

3. We aren't exactly at the point where we discuss the future.

4. I mean, it was just a kiss.

5. He's not my boyfriend...

6. ...right?

Bumps and Bruises

"Well, it wasn't Thor who gave them to me."

It's supposed to be a joke but she doesn't laugh,
probably because it's not funny.

When my father's fist made contact with my face,
it might as well have been a horse's hoof, it hurt as much.

I tell her the story like it happened to someone else
because that's easier than remembering out of my own eyes

how my father got so angry, I didn't even recognize him.
His face so twisted, like the face of some creature

you imagine under your bed instead of the face of the man

who gave you life and once promised to always protect you.

How he accused me of sneaking out with boys,

how he threw me down hard and I hit the nightstand.

How, when I tried to get back up to the soundtrack

of my mother's screams, I said something that

made him really angry because silence got me nowhere

but the very center of pain; what real damage could words do?

"You're right.

I have been sneaking out to see a boy."

And that was when

he punched me.

The Whys

"Why did you say those things?

Why didn't you just tell him

it's not what he thinks it is?"

I know that she's not blaming me

but rather trying to understand

why I poked a bear that already had

its mouth wrapped around my throat.

Did I go against some natural instinct

that other people have in their blood?

The answer alludes me,

like trying to catch smoke in my hands.

Maybe I just wanted it to happen,

the worst thing that could happen,

so I could stop holding my breath,

and it was somehow worse and also

not as bad as I thought it would be.

"You're staying with me

for the rest of the summer."

Who Am I

to argue?

Thirty-Seven Days

I leave for Colorado

in thirty-seven days,

just over a month.

For months, years,

lifetimes, I have imagined

the mountains, the quiet

university campus up in the hills

where my father's angry hands

can't reach me

but now, as I lay on Rachel's floor,

I think about Jason's blue eyes

and the way he kissed me

and about how much

I'm going to miss

the taste of his lips.

Boyfriend Things Jason Wells Does Even Though He's Not My Boyfriend

1. He texts me as soon as his eyes open

and seconds before he falls asleep

and randomly throughout the day,

often with emojis no one has ever used,

to chat about work and the ranch,

mostly checking in to make sure I'm okay,

that the cut in my eyebrow is healing.

2. He appears at Pretzel Mania every day

to try every flavor of pretzel that we sell

except the jalapeño one because he doesn't

like the taste of jalapeños but the chocolate chip

is his favorite so he buys one for me too

and we eat behind the counter when it's slow.

3. He tells me he has found new places for us

to explore at night but that he knows

I need time with Rachel on her floor

where I sleep every night instead of wandering.

4. He tells me that Thor misses me

and I wonder if he's really talking

about himself and I think he has to be

because this ache inside me can't just be me.

Outside Rachel's Window
Witching Hour #9

We're watching 10 Things I Hate About You

and eating caramel popcorn when someone

knocks on Rachel's window in the dead of night.

"I'm not looking,

you look."

"I'm not looking,

you look."

Through the thin pane of glass, a muffled voice

mixes with the noise of the summer wind.

"Bethany?

Rachel?

It's me."

Rachel doesn't know the sound of Jason's voice

the way I do, doesn't know who he means

when he says *me*.

I push aside white lace curtains, slide open glass,

see Jason grinning up at me, his white teeth

shining in the moonlight, his blue eyes so dark,

like the ocean at midnight, and I am ready to drown.

"I wanted to see you."

I decide immediately with a smack

of my metaphorical gavel that these are

the five best words in the English language,

all squished up against each other like that.

"Why didn't you text me?"

Rachel's face appears beside me

and she's wearing a grin, sort of like Jason

but not anything like Jason because this is her

I fucking told you so grin.

"Well, hello, Jason Wells."

He tips his hat at her

because he is a fucking cliché

but he's the cutest fucking cliché

that ever stepped foot in Watters.

"Mind if I steal Bethany for a second?"

Between the Houses

I don't remember I'm not wearing a bra

beneath my tank top until a stiff breeze

makes my nipples hard and I'm aware

of the pinch of them beneath the cotton of my shirt

and also aware of Jason's proximity,

so close I can feel his body heat, and I

cross my arms quick, but then I realize

I'm wearing shorts that are very short,

and Jason's eyes are attached to my legs

like they'll have to be surgically removed,

until he squeezes them shut because

apparently having them open at all

is just too much for him.

"You just saw me this afternoon."

I hope he can't hear my voice shake,

but it would break a Richter machine

so he probably hears it, but he pretends not to.

"I miss seeing you at night.

I always want to be around you."

And that makes me queasy and excited

in this weird jumble in my stomach

because of course I always want to be

around him too but those thirty-seven days

which are actually now thirty-one

are ticking in my head like a kitchen timer,

drowning out the beat of my own heartbeat

as Jason steps closer.

More Whys

Why

does he have to smell so good,

like cologne and the air freshener

in his truck and clean laundry?

Why

does he have to feel so good

when he settles those big hands

on my hips?

Why

do I have to feel this way

when he presses me gently

against the side of the house

and kisses me?

What She Knows

Rachel is watching me like she's waiting

for something to happen but I don't know

what that something is.

We're making steak quesadillas for her parents

but Rachel is doing more staring than preparing

and it's starting to feel like spiders under my skin.

"Would you stop that?"

Rachel shrugs, doesn't look away, in fact

leans a little closer, inspecting me like cells

under a microscope, and I don't know what she'll find.

"You look happy, Bethany."

I stop chopping raw steak, knife tip pressed

to cutting board, fingers pink, searching for purchase.

"I...I just..."

We have switched roles, and now I'm staring

while she chops vegetables, and I feel like

she's performed a magic trick on me, *abracadabra*.

"It's okay to really like him."

The casual way she says it makes me think

she doesn't understand what's going on here,

but I know she does, because Rachel always

understands, lives inside my head, a tenant

to my worst thoughts, and she knows the truth,

but for some reason, her mouth is speaking words

that refuse to synchronize with the situation.

"No, it's not."

There is not a pause, hesitation, interruption

in her movements, and I know I was wrong

for thinking she didn't understand when it's clear

she understands more than I do.

Thor Part II

Jason lets me ride Thor,

or rather, Jason makes me ride Thor

because it definitely wasn't my idea,

but here I am sitting atop of him,

black as night, with Jason's blue eyes

trained on me and his mouth making

these little noises that Thor seems to

understand, some horse language

that I'm not fluent in.

I grip the reins tight, sway back and forth

as Jason leads Thor out into the pasture

where he moves lazily, much like his master.

Jason informs me that Thor is fast

as lightning when he wants to be,

and I sincerely hope that Zeus

isn't up on Mount Olympus,

thinking it would be hilarious

to send forth lightning right now.

We trot because I made it very clear

to Jason and to Thor that if there is

an utterance of the word *gallop*,

I'm going home.

A nice, slow, leisurely pace.

And when it's over, and Jason

has wrapped his hands around my

hip bones to lift me off the saddle,

like this is the eighteenth century

and I'm a lady in skirts, he kisses me.

A nice, slow, leisurely pace.

My Father

has had almost a year to get used

to the information I handed him:

I was leaving for Colorado in August,

I would not be coming back in the fall,

I would not be seeing him ever again—

but he has had no time to get used

to my packed bags sitting beside our front door

like a joke: why did the duffel cross the road?

The flimsy cardboard boxes have been

stacked in my room since the day I got my

acceptance letter, eager to be taken to Colorado

or be left to the mercies of my parents,

but this is not boxes that will be unpacked

somewhere my father will never see.

This is my everyday clothes in tote bags,

my toothbrush in a hard-plastic case

next to my half-empty bottle of shampoo

and even though I'm not sneaking out,

not running while the sun is down,

I still find myself packing quick,

my fingers getting stuck on things

not normally handled in such haste

but no amount of hurry can keep away

the shape of my father in the doorway,

a foreboding outline of what was once

strength, paternity, love,

and what scares me the most is the fact

that my father isn't drunk, or at least

not as drunk as he would be at two a.m.,

when his first reaction would be to wound,

but I know there was whiskey in his coffee

this morning and gin in his glovebox for break.

But he doesn't have the heady sweat stink

of alcohol. His feet are steady, firmly planted

and his eyes, the most startling bit by far,

are clear and sharp, tightening on my bags,

scattered between us, where I dropped them

unslung, unloaded, like landmines,

barbed wire fencing, trip wires that he steps over

with sure feet, and I know without the sting of

experience, that his fists will be worse when

he really means it.

Scars

What I said to my father when he hit me

that night like a storm wasn't bravery.

It was madness or something worse

and now that it's the light of day,

I shield myself from the tornado,

hands over my head, bent at the waist

eyes squeezed shut

because the bruises and cuts he left me

with the last time we stood in this house

together haven't healed yet, and I don't know

if I can take anymore and I am a coward,

even when I'm pretending I'm not.

But just like last time, my father doesn't

find me with his fists first, he finds me

with his hands clasped around my arms

but this time when he shoves me, it isn't

into the furniture, it's out the front door,

and I trip on the doorframe onto the bags

I unburdened, that soften my landing.

The Dome
Witching Hour #10

Jason is giddy tonight, and I don't think

it's because he finally finished trying

all the flavors at Pretzel Mania

even though the caramel apple pretzel

is totally a reason to be giddy.

He's vibrating with excitement

and maybe a little nervousness,

and I marvel at his slightly clammy hand

in mine because this is not the boy

who looked me in the eye and asked

why not? the night we met.

"Oh, you asshole!"

We are standing in an observatory,

staring up through a domed glass ceiling

that offers an unimpeded, monstrous view

of countless twinkling stars, a telescope

right in the center, taller than me or Jason,

pointed up at the dome, the goddamn dome.

"I can't fucking believe

you have an observatory."

Like something out of a futuristic sci-fi film,

the glass dome splits, and we're standing

in the open air, humid and warm,

but not unbreathable, and Jason sits

beneath the telescope, grins up at me

like a little kid pulling his first prank,

and I want to kiss his face right off.

"I couldn't just hand you

all of my secrets

that very first day."

And I understand his words like some kind of

twisted inside joke because he asked me

that night about my father, and the reason

I wander Watters, and I didn't tell him

because he was absolutely nobody to me

and here he was this whole time,

holding a secret of his own.

"You're such a liar."

It's an insult given affectionately

as I sit on the floor with him and

press my face into his neck, wishing

on every star above us that I could

take him with me when I go.

Under the Stars

It's such a cliché,

moonlight on skin,

meeting for the first time

under the stars like

we're Romeo and Juliet

in hushed whispers

and even as he's on top

of me, pressing me down

into the floor, too hard

against the sharp corners

of my bones, even with the

blanket spread beneath me,

I'm wondering if he's brought

other girls here, if he's touched

them this way under the open sky,

gliding his fingers up the inside

of one thigh while I unclothe him

because I am a very specific brand

of desperate that doesn't seem

to have a name.

I have wanted boys and their boy parts

but I have never wanted to taste

their sounds so much that my fingers

ache, like the need is trying to escape

somehow, and it does, in a whimper

as I take off my clothes, bare myself

to Jason Wells and the constellations.

Jason is responsible, gentle,

as desperate as I am,

of that I'm certain.

Unknown Places

While I cannot—by any stretch

of the imagination of the English

language, taught to me in classrooms

and textbooks—call myself a virgin,

there are parts of me that haven't

been touched in the exact way that

Jason Wells is now touching them.

He translates my body into a veritable buffet

of flavors on fingertips and between thighs.

The taste of me on his tongue as he swipes

it up and round and inside, until he yanks

an orgasm from my limbs like it's

something to be stolen from closed fists.

And in this same way, I begin to map

the lines of him like a delicacy, just for me

and my lips and my tongue

and the very back of my throat,

unchartered territory, an arrow pointing

straight to the lost city of El Dorado.

Tangy salt transferred from shoulder

and neck and ear into my waiting mouth

to the discerning nerves on the tip

of my tongue, straight to my bloodstream.

The bright, hot sizzle of a second orgasm

interpreted as middle of the night pyrotechnics

that detonate along my veins,

burning, until I can taste it like bitter

apple skin as I pant and scream and fall.

The sharp bite and pop of

his euphoric groan in my ear

and the gentle way he teaches

me the exact pronunciation of

"I'm going to come.

I'm going to come.

I'm going to come."

This Is the Part

where I am supposed to put a crack in the

perfect stained-glass moment of this night,

where I am supposed to press my hand to Jason's

naked skin, glittering in the exposed starlight,

where I am supposed to tell him that when I go

in twenty-four days, it will be for good,

where I am supposed to stop being selfish and

let the truth boil from my mouth to scald us,

where I am not supposed to memorize every line of him

but instead walk out the door and never look back,

where I am not supposed to fall in love with him

because it'll leave us both in scattered pieces.

Even More Whys

"Why haven't you told Jason

you can't be with him once you're gone?"

Rachel always asks the questions

I don't want to answer, and I wish

I could say I didn't know why, but I know why.

I know that if I had told him when we first met

that I was leaving, going to Colorado

to get lost in the unfamiliar scent of somewhere else,

and that I wasn't planning on staying in touch

or coming back for Thanksgiving and Christmas

or even answering a phone call from an Oklahoma

area code, that he never would have done with me

what he did last night.

He wouldn't have kissed me, taken me to his observatory, quietly whispered that he was pretty sure he was falling in love with me when he pressed inside.

"You're making a huge mistake."

It Finally Happens

fourteen days before I'm set to get in my car

and drive away without looking back.

Jason and I are cuddled in his bed watching a movie,

his breath on the back of my neck and my whole body warm

because I'm always warm, warm enough to sweat,

when I'm plastered to him like this.

"I was thinking that in the fall we could take a trip,

you know, somewhere where the leaves change colors."

All the warmth from him seeps out through

the ends of my fingers until I'm certain he'll see

that my hands and lips have gone blue and stiff.

"About that..."

I'm already forcing my way out of his arms

because if he has them around me, I won't be able to say

what I need to. I won't be able to get it out.

I'll cave and tell him that he can have me forever.

"Look

I've always had a plan, for as long as I can remember, and that plan means getting out of Watters, it means running away and never looking back and, well, I'm not planning on coming back to Watters ever, not as long as I live, and if I'm never coming back then that means we can't..."

"But it's not just a long-distance relationship, is it? It's a relationship where we only see each other if you come all the way to Colorado and what about after I graduate? I don't even know where I'll be then..."

"I don't want to figure it out. I want to be free, and I know that might sound mean, but it's the truth. I can't have anything tying me here..."

"I just..."

“I’m sorry.”

One Last Why

"Why did you sleep with me then?"

Girls

I am a teenage girl who went to public school

and had friends who were also girls and

who lost her virginity at seventeen to a boy I

dated for almost a year before I told him yes.

I have heard the stories that get passed around

over tears at the lunch table and runny mascara

in the bathroom. I know that sometimes, boys say

what they have to say to get a girl to sleep with them.

I know about boys who made promises of forever

if they could just get it once, an exchange of goods,

an *I love you* for a trip to third base at the very least,

but this is not that, please don't think that this is that.

In Rachel's quiet expression from the other side of

her room, where I am dripping on her cream carpet,

shivering in the underwear I put on in hopes that Jason

would take them off while it stormed outside,

I see that she isn't so sure that isn't exactly what she thinks,

but I swear on the gravestone of every person who is buried

in Watters Cemetery that when Jason slid his

hands along my skin, I wasn't thinking about what came next.

I was thinking about feeling him, knowing him,

about how everything about him felt like the right answer

to every question I've ever asked myself, even the one

that goes *what the hell are you going to do now?*

It didn't occur to me not to be an asshole when Jason

was breathing into my mouth. It didn't occur to me

to do anything but let him fuck me, even when I knew

I shouldn't dig my claws into him any deeper than they were.

No Whys

Rachel

doesn't ask me

any more questions.

Instead,

all she says is

"Bethany,

you're a fucking idiot."

Part Four
Home

Freedom

I'm free.

Like a mantra, every day

for the last month, over and over,

the words live under my tongue.

Every time Rachel sends me

a news article from her dorm in

Stillwater about Jason meeting success,

always written in lazy sports metaphors.

Every time I lay in my extra-long twin bed

with the same stars above me as the stars

above Jason's observatory and wonder

in an aching, angry, split-open kind of way

if he's taking another girl there and

spreading her out on the floor.

Every time I touch myself while wishing

it was his rough hands and balmy skin

under the blanket I bought brand new,

covered in gold and silver stars.

Every time I need a reminder that there is

a reason for this ache, the twinge I still feel

in the vicinity of my ribs every morning when

I wake up and remember that he hasn't texted.

Every time I need it to take the shape of truth

in my mouth instead of the sound of an excuse.

A Phone Call From Mom

"Sweetie, hi, I know it's late

but it's your father. He's in the hospital

and they're pretty sure this is it. They don't think he's going to
make it. I know it'll take you a while to get here

and that's fine

but I think you should come. I know he hasn't been good to you,
to either of us,

but I think you should come say goodbye, if nothing else
because I don't want you to

regret it."

The Thing About Watters

is that I never hated it.

Yes,

all the businesses besides J-Mart

turn over their CLOSED signs

before the stars have even had a

chance to sprinkle themselves

across the sky.

Yes,

everybody knows everybody in that

annoying, small-town way that is

only charming to people who live in

cities where no one knows you're dead

until the smell drifts into the hallway.

Yes,

the town is split right down the middle,

a clean separation between upper and

lower class that has a disgusting effect

on the way its residents treat each other,

with Wells Ranch presiding over us all

like a palace in the distance.

But no,

it's not Watters' fault that my father

resides within its limits or that my father

is now dying or that I am so fucked up

that it's barely been two months and I am

packing a bag, eager to return.

Driving Part II

I have what feels like infinite time

to sit in my mind on the drive from

Fort Collins to Watters,

an eleven-hour trip, seven hundred miles

that I cover in one fell swoop after

waking with a sinking feeling I couldn't identify

to listen to my mother's voicemail in the dark

because the sun wasn't up yet, and my mother's

voice was so small and still so desperate

like someone whispering to a 9-1-1 operator

through a tin can and a piece of knitting yarn,

just barely audible over my roommate's snoring.

I drive until my foot cramps on the gas pedal

and stop at a McDonald's on the highway for

a Big Mac and an arguably clean bathroom

and it makes me wish I had emptied my piggy bank

for a plane ticket because all this time in the car

with my brain and my body has given me too much time

to snap back to reality, like a dream fading into memory,

to recognize my own feet running back to Watters like

I didn't fight with my bare hands to get the hell away.

Infinite Whys

Ask me why

I'm rushing back to

Watters.

Regret

Regret is a bewildering animal

because of course it's impossible

to know what you will regret

when it's happening, like eating

something that's been sitting out too long

and waiting to see if it will make you sick.

It lurked in the corners of rooms

as I packed my things to ditch Watters,

sat in the passenger seat as I drove out of town

because no matter how eager my feet

were to tread new ground, my lungs

ready for a new kind of oxygen, some other

part of me knew the chances of him dying,

of him killing her, of my being buried alive

under the fear of my father and his fists

if I turned around.

I counted the days, waited for my new life

to scare away the threat of regret that lived

and boiled inside me at leaving Jason behind,

a sunburn refusing to heal and instead, aching,

and it will be the nail in my coffin.

New

Back in the 90s, Watters

was a farm town, a tall-grass polygon

with farms from border to border,

half a dozen churches,

and a pharmacy on the corner,

just a gas station that sold cheap coffee.

But now on Main Street

there's a McDonald's,

a Starbucks, a development

named Watters Haven that appeared

as the farms started to die, shut down by

mass-producing industries,

leaving open land

with For Sale signs

large and looming,

so even though I've always seen horses

in pastures as I drove down the road

or spotted cows, donkeys, sheep,

I have never seen one

in the middle of the road

like there is now,

a pitch-black sloped outline

grazing at the edge of the concrete

right in front of my car.

Thor Part III

Coming to a stop on Franklin Street, the road in
Watters with the highest speed limit, is like jumping
into a shark tank: close your eyes, hope for the best
because the sharks won't stop their snapping for you.

The horns honk louder than my own pulse in my ears
and the joints of my fingers where they're wrapped
around my steering wheel, threatening to crack under
the pressure of highway gravity and sheer terror.

We're on the edge of Wells Ranch, because if you're
anywhere in Watters, you're on the edge of Wells Ranch,
long acres from the barn where I first met Thor, but

I know his eyes and the length of his mane

and the lazy way that he moves when he doesn't

feel threatened, even by cars on this four-lane road,

screaming past at sixty miles an hour, missing him but

still stirring up air that flutters the tips of his hair,

and I watch it all through my windshield, feel the rock

of each car that bolts past the flicker of my hazard lights,

pulsing rhythmically on the thick, round bones above

Thor's hooves, frozen in horrified terror.

Thor has taken one step into the still-moving lane,

hoof crossing over the broken white stripe,

a car passing so close to him the muscles under

the skin of his shoulders bunch in a cringe.

I grit my teeth because even a scream through

a windshield and rolled-up windows and two tons

of metal would probably be enough to startle him

and there are too many horrors in my mind to let that happen.

There is a lull in the traffic, most likely a red light

somewhere down the road, only seconds before the

cars of the intersecting street will meet us, a split second

to go against every natural instinct I possess and step

into the road, my sneaker skidding on microscopic

pieces of loose concrete, and when I throw my hands up

in front of an oncoming car that flashes its brights at me

like I'm standing here for my own enjoyment,

a thought runs through my head: I am going to die today

and for a fucking horse that belongs to my theoretical ex, and

I don't know a damn thing about horses except for the quiet

reassurances Jason offered me that day in the pasture

but I do know that if Thor doesn't want to move,

I will not be able to make him by sheer force,

as his center of gravity is heavier than my own

by literal metric tons with no harness slung about him.

I try to tug him by the end of the nose, the tips of his mane,

make clucking noises with my tongue, beckon him toward me

with wild hand gestures as if he's a dog and I'm an idiot

but despite my clear and apparent incompetence,

Thor still comes to me, still whinnies and follows, and

if ever there was a moment where I might feel some validation

that I have any worth as a human being, it is this one

until Jason's voice carries over to us on the dying wind.

Jason Wells Part II

And I guess, really, I hear his boots in the grass

before I hear his voice over the sound of traffic

impatiently picking up speed on Franklin Street

but it's his voice that makes the world seem too

bright, somehow overexposed, until I could almost

forget where I'm standing, where I've ended up.

"Dammit, Thor,

what the hell were you thinking?

You could have gotten killed."

With my back turned, his familiar tones set off a kind

of craving for him to be speaking to me, even with angry

words, so long as the words are coming in my direction.

I consider, in the seconds of silence that follow his

reprimand, making a run for my car, hazards still beating

against concrete, because facing my dying father

has to be easier than this.

"I'm surprised he followed you.

He's a stubborn pain in the ass.

Took off like nobody's business

when one of the grooms lost his hold.

But then, he's always liked you."

There's such affection curled around the words

that I could die and decompose at his feet, melt into

the grass and not have to go in search of a response.

Ask me why I have my back turned still, and I will say

that, just like keeping a secret, the second I turn and

see him, I will have to admit that this is all real.

"What are you doing here?"
The tinge of affection that has colored his words in

an odd indifference has shifted into something harder

but not what I was expecting, not shock or sadness

or some version of the torment in my own blood, but

an accusation because I didn't keep my end of the bargain.

"My dad is sick."

He knows, of course, about the tumor but this is my way

of saying that he is actually much more than sick.

"I came to see him before…"

He circles me like a vulture, but I can only watch

his shoes, lost in the hip-high Indian Grass,

the ones he once told me were made of stingray

and to me, that sounded like fantasy, like having

shoes made of unicorn skin, because I can't watch him.

"I'll come with you."

Unexpected

It's the thing that finally gets me

to look up and up and up at Jason.

It's almost full dark now, the sky

a heavy purple weight around him

and my headlights still cascading

across the concrete, and the distant

sound of my stereo playing into the

open air across the wide field to reach us

and Thor giving a grunt of impatient

displeasure somewhere behind my back.

"Why?"

He gets darker with the sky, until he's a

silhouette in the middle of a field with

Jason's height and shoulders and shape

but my eyes convince me I can still make out

that expression on his face, like an image

left on your retinas when the light's gone out.

Even though I put his heart into a blender,

Jason is still trying to save me, and this time

I might let him.

"Because I don't want you to be alone."

Hospital

My mother is a humped figure over my father's hospital bed,

hand over his as he breathes unevenly around the cancer

in his lungs and the cancer that has moved to remote parts

of his body until his body is more cancer than man.

The beast that is regret whispers in my ear at the shape of her,

the only thing that had the power to keep me tethered to this

place, but I severed that binding nonetheless with my eyes

closed so that I wouldn't have to see her like this, whatever it is.

It is strange that I'm standing in this place, awash in white-

blue light and the language of machines monitoring my father

when he's the only reason I'm not here, if I'm being honest.

I hate him, even when he's dying and can't hurt me, and

the me that wanted to see him before the end so that the beast

won't gnaw at my bones forever is the same me that wants, with

an ugly satisfaction that might make me more monster than girl,

to watch him take his last breath because it's a romantic notion,

to feel revenge.

No Apologies

My father reaches the surface, unburied,

sometime around three in the morning

and I'm the only one awake because

that's something that hasn't worn off,

like a freckle that appears on the back

of your hand halfway through your life.

Mom's soft head lulls on the other side

of the bed, over the armrest of a chair,

and Jason's whole body is bent onto a

recliner by the window, his hands tucked

under his cheek like he's a little kid in a

movie who's faking at being asleep.

"How's Colorado?"

That he could ask such a question when

his own actions are the open palms that

pushed me away from Watters and Mom

and him makes me wish I had stayed in

my dorm because then his angry words

would be the last ones that ever hit my ears.

"Colorado is amazing."

Colorado is clean air and clear skies, but being

there is the ground cleaved in two, one half

of me being tugged back here by the boy

in the corner with the kind eyes, the longhorn

belt buckle, the catch-you-by-surprise smile.

The other half: a contented sort of emptiness.

"You're free now.

You'll—

hoarse

wheeze

be free."

In the glow of the TV and the display

on his machines, counting out every one of

his heartbeats, I can see every slice of pigment

in his brown eyes that he gave me, and in a

split second that seems drawn out for years

and years, I see my father of before,

the perimeter of him traced in front of me

like the last lingering image of someone in a

dream, someone you know you don't know

but you still feel pulled toward, like they were

once important and could be again, and I know

without him having to translate what he means,

with those knowing eyes, so focused and clear,

eyes that I remember and recognize but have

forgotten in that way we forget people before

our minds are old enough to form them into

memories. He doesn't mean I'll be free of

Watters. He means I'll be free of him.

Before

There weren't piggyback rides

or paternal cheers from the bleachers

but there were after-school trips

for drive-thru burgers

and precious handholds

to cross the street.

There wasn't constant bragging

that's my daughter

or trips to carnivals

zoos or lakes for fishing

but there were

hugs before bed

matching grape sodas

from the J-Mart vending machine.

I never knew that Hollywood perfect

father with the heartfelt smile

but I knew my dad:

quiet, sincere, safe.

My dad is not lying in a hospital bed.

My dad was devoured long ago

by cancer cells

and sticky brown liquor

and an anger so acute

it destroyed us all.

Wells Ranch Part III

My transition from the hard-plastic hospital chair

to a bed at Wells Ranch is not much more than the

flowing of bright lights and murmured words between

my mother and Jason, while the sky is still dark outside,

the warmth of Jason's hands as he leads me to his truck,

the scent of hay and mud and his air freshener as I strive

to keep my eyes open because I'm a master of staying awake,

but everything from my neck up is a heavy weight, and

Jason's nearness is a drug pulling me under until I feel

the soft cotton of sheets below me, fresh from the dryer,

with no idea if my feet brought me there or not.

Mr. Wells

Voices far away yet close enough for me to make out

the punch of syllables bring me back to the surface,

where things are sharp again and have color and also

the smell of coffee and something smoky, and I

follow the scent of homemade food like a cartoon

following wavy aroma lines because I have eaten

nothing but food made in a microwave since I moved.

Jason captures all of my attention, in fresh clothing,

skin pink from the heat of a recent shower, and I'm

moving toward him by some force far beyond myself

when another figure materializes in my periphery,

pulling out a stool from the kitchen island for me to sit

and placing a bowl of brown beef stew in my hand

that makes me question how many meals I've slept through.

"I'm Malcolm Wells."

The introduction is unnecessary, not just because

Malcom Wells is as famous as Wells Ranch and

because of the night he helped me with my car, a night

I'm sure he doesn't remember as he probably has

a forgotten inventory of broken-down individuals,

Watters citizens that he's rescued from distress,

but because I know his face from memorizing Jason's.

Piercing blue eyes, dark wavy hair, that look of protection

with a paternal edge that is a strange visitor.

"Thank you for letting me stay

and for the food.

I'll head home as soon as I can."

They move at the same time, practiced in the art

of hospitality and comfort, Malcom putting a hand

on my shoulder while Jason pours coffee in my mug.

"You should stay.

Your mother called.

Everything is okay for now.

Get some rest."

Surrounded in their compassion like

a heated blanket of Wells men, I feel unsteady.

"Thank you."

Lover

There are no words, not outright,

of forgiveness or otherwise,

but when Jason's mug is dry,

he leaves the kitchen and I follow,

and perhaps it's wishful thinking,

the culmination of so much wanting,

that makes me shut the door behind me

closing us into the space of his bedroom,

that want for being close to him, near him,

in whatever form that takes,

beginning to buzz in my head

like an angry beehive.

"I thought it might be hard

for you to go home.

Are you okay?"

I don't have an answer for him because

it is just as hard to be here at Wells Ranch

as it is to go home but for different reasons

filed under the same heading.

I thought I knew in uncertain moments and

hard-fought days what it meant to not be okay.

When my father raised a hand to my mother or to me,

when he left behind bruises I had to explain to teachers,

when his monstrous anger haunted me

and left me tiptoeing around my life,

left me feeling like I was locked in a cage

with knuckles bloodied from trying to escape.

That was just a taste of not okay

and here I am, choking on the main course.

I was prepared for my dad to die, and held

the fact with careful hands, unsure what to do with it.

He outlived his life expectancy by six months

but I never thought the day would be wrapped

in the wounds I still have from leaving Jason,

in the ache I feel at having him so near,

so full of easy forgiveness and mercy

for my transgressions against him.

Death is hard enough without Jason's

aliveness here to muck it all up.

I sob and Jason has his arms around me

in record time, gold metal in sympathy

and I want to push away because

how can he be so good?

He soothes me, rubs my back,

leads me to the bed, where I perch on his lap

and let him stroke my hair like I'm a child

as the tears dry against my eyelashes.

His hands slow like the feet of a runner

as the race comes to an end. It'll be over soon

this affliction of confused sadness,

the very tips of his fingers

whispering over the softness of my face

as he brushes my salt wet hair back

behind my ear, and I feel heavy,

weighty, all of my limbs full.

"I love you."

Come Back to Me

The shift is so quiet, I almost don't know

if I meant for it to happen or not, or if

somehow it was my body's idea to press

just an inch closer, my cheek against the

hollow above his clavicle and my skin

finding that his cheeks are wet too,

sliding along mine until I taste the salt

against my lips, clinging to his jaw

and then it happens fast.

My mouth is open against his and his

tongue tastes like coffee and his hands

curl around my waist so tight I could bruise,

pulling me to straddle him, pressing my hips

down to meet his, like we've been starving,

hungry, so hungry, for lips and hands.

We're naked so fast, his undressed skin

fevered against mine and I wait for him

to lay me down on his sheets that smell like

him, but he settles me back in his lap, limbs

a tangle of elbows and thighs, pushes up

into me and sighs against my chest.

"Come back to me."

My nails bite into his shoulders like the

pop of split plum skin, leave crescent scars

like maybe I can mark him and memorize him

and claim him while still letting him go,

force him into remaining untouched and mine

and as far away from me as he can get all at once.

"I can't."

He whimpers, groans, sounds that will live in

the drums of my ears until the day I die.

"I love you."

He's said it twice now. I've said it not at all.

But every inch of my body is screaming it

at him in words so loud I'm hoarse without

ever opening my mouth.

"Come back to me."

I close my eyes,

arch my back,

shout up at the ceiling.

Watters

Jason Wells is Watters.

He's

the color of the sky at two a.m.,

the smell of the fountain as it splashes over,

the feel of a cool breeze against my sweaty skin,

the sound of the alarm on the pretzel oven,

the quiet of an empty chapel on the highway,

the taste of hash browns and mango salsa.

And I can't leave him.

I can't.

I can't.

He drags me under, holds me still,

until I'm gasping and desperate to drown

in him, rasps against my throat one more time

"I love you."

The Next Few Days

My father dies thirty-three hours later, the

three of us sentried around his bed as he

takes his last breath, and there is something

sickening and hazy about knowing I was the

last person he spoke to and looked in the eye

before the coma set in that he would live in

until his body finally gave up the fight.

Three days later, we have a small funeral

and bury my father in Watters Cemetery,

in a small plot that my mother tells me

has room for all three of us, but I pray my

body will never be put to rest here, in Watters.

My mother is oddly calm, assuring me as I

pack my bags again that she'll be okay, that

she has a plan, and I assure her that I'll be back

soon, leaving behind a few things as collateral,

one of Jason's t-shirts and a picture of Rachel

in a frame on the wall, so she knows I mean it

because I can't keep the promise I made

when I left Watters. I'm going back to

Colorado, but I'll return for Thanksgiving

and in time to help her buy a Christmas tree

and in the heat of the summer to swim in

Rachel's pool and maybe sleep on her floor.

Like a flimsy boomerang, I will come back

to Jason's waiting arms and my mother's lonely

house and Rachel's smiling face because I hate

Watters but the people in it are home.

A Goodbye Kiss

Zoom in on my car parked in the U-shaped driveway

of Wells Ranch and Jason's hands buried in my hair,

his lips intending to be gentle, sweet, romantic

but instead devouring me against the side of my car.

"I'll see you soon."

And it *will* be soon, less than a month from now,

when Jason and Mr. Wells drive Thor to California,

where he has an appointment to become a daddy,

and when their business is done, they will diverge

somewhere around New Mexico so that Jason can visit

Colorado and introduce his scent to my bedsheets.

There will always be miles between us until I decide
where it is that I belong, but his road will always lead
to me and mine to him and we will find a way back to
each other, our paths connected instead of forked,
two rivers flowing from different ends into the same
ocean because they were always fated to meet.

Part Five
Anywhere

"Do You Hear That?"

Yes, I do hear it.

The whisper of the wind

on the tall stalks of yellow-gold

grass in this field in Kansas.

I once thought that Oklahoma

was the most boring place on Earth,

like drawing a stick figure with

No. 2 charcoal on a sheet of

wide-ruled notebook paper,

but Kansas is stale white bread

that someone forgot in the back

of the pantry until it's time to

make grilled cheese, and you won't

notice the texture anyway, so why not?

Kansas was not designed to be beautiful,

like the stretch of the Rockies,

blue and blue and blue, outlined

on every postcard and travel brochure

and it is not Oklahoma,

rich in the currency of its history,

filled with ancient animals

and campsites with log cabins,

a slow crawl down the highway

from a gas station casino,

a technicolor mishmash of

nature and something far uglier.

Kansas is useful, the geographic

center of the contiguous United States,

the birth place of Amelia Earhart,

the Arkansas River, and The Wizard of Oz.

A Scholar and a Gentleman

Four months ago, I graduated with a degree

in Agricultural Sciences because when my

guidance counselor asked me what I was

interested in, I delivered a speech as intricate

as a Union Address about the boyfriend I

left behind in Oklahoma and his black beast, Thor,

and his observatory that he told me wasn't an

observatory, until she begged me to stop and

told me that Agricultural Sciences might be useful

for me for when I move back to help with the ranch.

Only...

I never did move back to Watters.

Because the world is wide and full

of wonders, including the wonder that is

Malcolm Wells, who patiently listened

to Jason explain that he didn't want to take

over Wells Ranch, his birthright and apple of his eye.

He wanted us to start fresh, with Thor

and a mare named Hollyhock and the money

we'd both saved over the years for the day

when we would be right here,

holding hands in the middle of a wheat field,

imagining the house we're going to build.

Attached

Four years is a long time to go

without feeling someone's heart beat

under your ear as you lay on their bare chest

in the early gray light of September.

Now, when we venture into town

to stock up on groceries and Thor's

molasses treats, we move as a single unit,

from the house to the truck,

from the truck to the shop.

I sit in the middle of the bench as he drives so

I can feel the heat of him against me,

and he helps me out of the truck

when we park in the sun-baked parking lot

so he can feel me under his fingers

and remember that I'm here,

and we are together, and he is allowed to

touch me whenever and however he wants.

We collect interested looks

from people whose property

nestles against our own, and they start

calling us *the sweetie pies,*

though we are fairly certain that the name is meant

to be a secret and not something

we tease each other with as soon as we get home.

Forever

I walk my fingers across Jason's muscular chest

like the itsy bitsy spider as the autumn morning

begins to stretch into afternoon.

We climbed out of bed before dawn to take care

of Thor and answer emails and have breakfast

and then crawled right back into it.

Our body heat has settled a sheen across my skin

but I am far too stubborn to throw off the covers

or admit that being against him is intolerable.

I will burst into flames before I admit that.

"I was thinking…"

The last time he said this, we ended up pulling a

horse trailer across the state line and parking

it on a wheat field like we had a clue what we were doing.

"I don't like the sound of that."

He sets the box in the center of his chest,

approximately seven centimeters from the tip of my nose

and even this close, when the world would usually

turn into a blob with shadows and lines, I can still make

out the severe cut of a diamond, the shimmering silver band,

a robin's egg blue box, tipped in a white ribbon.

"You sure about that?"

Jason fucking Wells is a mirror ball of sharp angles,

boundless joy when he's alive in the fields, riding Thor

or fucking me on the hard dirt under our favorite tree,

solemn sadness when he presses his lips to my scars

or listens while I recount tails of infernos and caged

animals leaving cracks in the walls of my childhood home,

stern and unmovable in the midst of business transactions,

when people digest the smooth youthfulness of his skin and

think he will be an easy bullseye, a flimsy paper target,

and this version here, the one that asked *why not* and laughs

when I beg him to fill me and cocks one sharp eyebrow when

presenting me with an engagement ring

because he's certain I will say

"Yes."

And somewhere in the distance, under the whistle of the wind

and the soft grunts of Thor, running wild in the south pasture,

is the gentle conversation of Kansas mud

and the ripple of water.

About the Author

B. Randall has been a voracious romance reader since she stumbled upon a spicy book at the public library when she was fourteen. She has three traditionally published YA novels, over a dozen indie published works, and is a freelance editor who loves helping other indie authors produce their best work. When she's not writing, she's drinking fancy coffee with her friends, listening to the Toni and Ryan Podcast, and watching Formula 1 nonstop. She lives in Dallas with her husband.

Also by B. Randall

The Berserkr Gym Series

Come In With The Rain

Make It To Me

Take My Love

Find Me Here

Let Me Fall

Give Your Heart Away

The Vegas Duet

A Man After Midnight

Late Night Talking

Braving the Waves

Love Is an Open Door

Love in Slow Motion

Writing as Winter Randall

My Best Friend's Mate

The Vamp and I

Five Nights With The Fire Monster

King of the Fire Monsters

Snowed In With The Mountain Monster

Touched by the Shadow Creature

Minotaur Sugar Daddies

My Gargoyle Protector

www.ingramcontent.com/pod-product-compliance
Lightning Source LLC
Chambersburg PA
CBHW061111310726
48974CB00002B/488